Whoever You Are

Whoever You Are

Diana Hendry

h
Hodder
Children's
Books

First published in Great Britain in 2018
by Hodder Children's Books

The song Ma sings on page 125 is from 'A Red, Red Rose' by Robert Burns

3 5 7 9 10 8 6 4 2

A Catalogue record for this book is available from the British Library

ISBN 978 1 444 92478 7

Hodder Children's Books
A division of Hachette Children's Group
Part of Hodder & Stoughton
Carmelite House,
50 Victoria Embankment,
London, EC4Y 0DZ

An Hachette UK Company
www.hachette.co.uk

For Talia with love from Granny D

What the Seagull Saw

She was a Scottish seagull and she had a
particular route. First stop was *Dizzy Perch*,
a quite ridiculous house set high up among the
cliffs so that to live there was like living in the
clouds. There were a lot of rival gulls flying
around *Dizzy Perch*, not to mention gannets
and razorbills, daft puffins and serious fulmars.
But the family living there, the Coggins, were
generous with their crusts (particularly Titch).

When there was a shortage, this seagull –
let's call her Sibyl – would take a ride on a
gentle air current down to the harbour at
Starwater, the nearby village, where there
were always good pickings to be had from the

boats and the fishermens' nets.

Just beyond Starwater, there was a field with a handy fence post for Sibyl to stand on, balancing on one leg which she was good at. There was a caravan here, owned by a large and grumpy man, and there was also a chestnut horse. And oats. Oats that sometimes spilled and allowed Sibyl a small feast.

This was almost her daily route – *Dizzy Perch*, Starwater harbour, the field with the horse, and back to *Dizzy Perch*.

Goodness, this sounds like the beginning of a story . . .

Chapter 1

A Rival's Plan

In his shabby old caravan, Big Mac sat hunched over his telescope. He'd been sitting there all morning with first one eye, then the other, clamped to it, so that now he had sore eyes, a sore head and a very sore temper. *Dizzy Perch* was cloaked in a swirl of mist.

Not that it was the house Big Mac wanted to see. It was the family inside it and this morning there was not a single Coggin to be seen – not Ma, Pa, Oliver, Lottie, Titch or even the old 'un, Grandpa Coggin. Big Mac gave a snort that sent the caravan's resident spider scuttling for cover. What were they all doing? Big Mac had been spying on *Dizzy Perch* for the last three months.

Right now he would have been glad to see any of them, but most of all Pa Coggin. Pa – or, to give him his annoyingly grand title, Professor Amos Coggin – was Big Mac's old rival and Sworn Enemy.

Big Mac stomped out into the field. The caravan shook on its mooring. An old frying pan hung beside the front door, together with a worn metal ladle. Big Mac gave the pan three good whacks that rang across the field in the most satisfactory way and which, if he was lucky, would bring his sister Moll.

There were a great many things Moll was good at. Making Big Mac's tea. Listening to Big Mac's moans and groans. Washing Big Mac's jumpers, pants, and socks. Putting up with Big Mac's plans. Doing what Big Mac told her to do (though not without fuss). Combing the tangles out of Big Mac's hair. It was a pity she had one fault. And it was a big one: Moll cared more about her horse, Amber, than she did about Big Mac.

So now, even though Big Mac banged on the frying pan again and again and hollered 'Moll!

Moll!' she took not a blind bit of notice. He could see her over in the stable. As usual, she was busy grooming the creature, stroking its nose, crooning to it, lavishing the kind of love and care on the beast which by rights belonged to him, her brother.

Big Mac had to put on his wellies and stomp across the field to speak to her. It was April. It had been raining for days. The ground was quite deliciously squelchy. Big Mac was of the opinion that Moll should come when called. After all, who was it paid for her board and keep in the hayloft above the stable? And, more importantly, paid for Amber's board and keep, which was a lot more expensive.

Amber snorted a huff of breath at him from her soft, wet nose. Moll didn't bother looking up. She had the soft brushes out. Amber's chestnut coat glowed.

'How's the Sworn Enemy?' Moll asked, her face buried in Amber's side.

Why did she always have to mock? Big Mac wondered.

5

'Nowhere in sight,' he said icily. 'I suppose you'll be needing more oats soon,' he said pointedly. You had to remind her who was boss around here.

Moll sighed, put down her brush, gave Amber a last pat and a sugar lump, and came out of the stable.

'Telescope not working?' she asked.

'Too much mist to see,' said Big Mac. 'And nobody coming out.'

'Why don't you give up?' asked Moll. (This was a question she asked at least once a week.) 'Do something useful instead?'

'Revenge!' shouted Big Mac. 'Revenge will be very useful! Not to mention profitable!'

The rain had started up again. They headed back to the caravan.

'I'll make us some hot chocolate,' Moll said, knowing that once the word 'revenge' was uttered, her brother would be off on one of his rants. 'It'll be soothing,' she added. But it was too late. Big Mac had gone into Instant Rant mode.

'At school,' he began, 'who became house captain when it should have been . . . ?'

'You,' Moll offered obligingly.

'And at university, who won the chemistry prize and the physics prize and the post-graduate fellowship when it should have been . . . ?'

'You, again,' said Moll, adding extra sugar to the hot chocolate.

'And then,' said Big Mac, his head in his hands, a kind of sob in his voice, 'who got the girl?'

'Umm, Maisie?' said Moll. 'You'd probably have gone off her.'

'Never!' declared Big Mac.

'You could be holed up in that crazy house with three awful children,' said Moll, putting the mug of hot chocolate in front of him. 'Think about it. Would that make you happy?'

Big Mac banged the table with his fist, making both Moll and the hot chocolate jump. 'You just don't understand, do you?' he yelled. 'Why d'you think he's moved them into that "crazy house", as you call it? Miles from anywhere. Miles from anyone.'

'I haven't the slightest idea,' said Moll, licking the last of the chocolate from the spoon. 'Maybe they like it up there in the clouds.'

'Idiot!' said Big Mac. 'It's to keep them hidden away.'

'But why?' asked Moll.

'Why?' repeated Big Mac. Rage seemed to make him swell up like a balloon.

'Why? Because that man, that clever Clever-Clogs Coggin . . .'

'Your Sworn Enemy . . .'

'Yes. My Sworn Enemy has discovered a new medicine. He's taken the research I began—'

'Before you gave up and took to feeling sorry for yourself—'

'Before I had a chance, or the funding—'

'Or the persistence . . .'

'Or Maisie. Or the luck. I've read about it. I recognise my own idea. And now they're saying it's going to be the new antibiotic, just when that's what we all need most because the

8

old ones have stopped working and now if he manages to develop it, he'll sell it to the drug companies for millions and millions of pounds – unless I do something about it. Claim what's rightfully mine. That's why I've got to find out where he's going.'

'I don't understand,' said Moll. 'Why would he hide his family in *Dizzy Perch* and then go off somewhere else?'

'I know he's going off somewhere because I've seen that yellow helicopter flying about. That's his friend, Joe. Joe who was once my friend.'

'Like Maisie was once your girl?' said Moll.

'Don't you be mocking me,' said Big Mac. 'I've got a plan. Clever-Clogs Coggin has a secret laboratory somewhere. I need to find it. That, my dear, dear sister, is The Plan.'

'Plan Six,' said Moll wearily. 'I don't think I want to be involved in any more of your plans. I think jealousy has messed up your brain.'

'And horse craziness has messed up yours!' snarled Big Mac. 'Don't want to be involved in any more of my plans, eh? Just want to go gallopy, gallopy. Just want to ride far away. Just you and Amber. Pity you need me, isn't it? No me. No oats, no hay, no stable, no vet, no nothing.'

'OK, OK! I'll fix the telescope. I'll give you a haircut. I'll make an apple tart. I'll wash your pants.'

Big Mac sprawled back in his chair, his belly growing fat just with the thought of apple tart. 'That's more like it,' he said. 'But you might be too busy.'

'Too busy?'

'Yes. Busy with Plan Six.'

'Your plan.'

'No, sister dear. Our plan. Didn't you say Amber needed new shoes?'

'Our plan,' said Moll. 'What d'you want me to do?'

Big Mac's smile was one you wouldn't want turned on you. 'Well, it's about those children,' he said, 'the Coggin children: Oliver, Lottie and Titch. You like children, don't you?'

'I like horses,' said Moll.

'Ah yes, but children can be just as interesting don't you think? I mean, I know they only have two legs instead of four and lack tails and can't run nearly as fast, but they can talk, can't they? Talking seems quite an important talent to me.'

'You want me to talk to them? The children?'

'That's a really good idea,' said Big Mac in his sweetest tones. 'Why didn't I think of that?'

'And find out where their pa – I mean, the Sworn Enemy – is going?'

'Exactly. Couldn't have put it better myself.'

'And how am I to do that? I suppose you expect me just to climb up to *Dizzy Perch* and knock on the door?'

'Umm, I think you'll need a better idea than that! I was thinking that you might bring one or other of the children here. Just for a little visit. What d'you think?'

'I think you're out of your mind,' said Moll.

'Do you now?' said Big Mac, grinning nastily. 'What a shame if Amber were to get a bit skinny, don't you think? Now, how about setting up the telescope for me? The mist must have lifted by now. Maybe the family will emerge. You can take a good look at them, dear.'

'Please don't *dear* me,' said Moll. But it was the only protest she could make. Big Mac watched as she swivelled the angle of the telescope, and set the sight ring to the right place.

'There!' she said, taking the first look.

It was impossible to look up at *Dizzy Perch* without somehow feeling excited. Enlarged by the telescope's eye, the house's wonkiness – its ridiculous balconies, its flapping half-hinged shutters, the funicular railway that clanged noisily up and down the cliff whenever a Coggin wanted to go down to the beach – made Moll smile, made her think that it must be lovely living up there as a family with a whole beach as your garden instead of in a field with a horrible brother who had an even horribler plan.

Big Mac was right. The mist had lifted. Moll could see Ma sitting out on her balcony. She looked as if she was reading a book. Two little

Coggins were riding down to the beach on the funicular railway. An old man who must be the Grandpa stood on the rocks at the back of the house, and looked as if he was talking to the birds. A middle-sized boy sat on an old crate and looked as if he might be whittling a piece of wood. There was something about the way he sat there, hunched up over his piece of wood that made Moll think he looked either sad or lonely or both.

There was no sign of the Sworn Enemy.

Chapter 2

The Rules

Up in *Dizzy Perch*, on a bright April morning when the swallows were swirling round the wonky tower and a full tide was glinting down below, Pa Coggin called a family meeting.

The night before he'd pinned a notice on the kitchen door. It said:

FAMILY POWWOW
SITTING ROOM
9 A.M. SHARP

Someone, possibly Titch, had drawn an elephant with a very long trunk showering a mouse with water on the notice.

14

Someone else, possibly Ma, had crossed out 9 A.M. SHARP and written *How about 10 a.m. blunt? Ha ha ha!*

But now it was after ten and apart from Pa, the only other being in the sitting room was Biggles the cat, snugged up nicely in the softest of the three sofas.

Pa had lined up the other sofas, thrown some cushions on the floor, and arranged a tall stool for himself with a table next to it on which lay his latest Goodbye Speech and the current list of 'Rules to be Obeyed'. Out in the hall, his bags – a big yellow holdall, the tough leather case containing his new scientific equipment, plus a box of groceries – were all ready and waiting. Waiting to be sent down on the funicular railway to the beach, where in exactly an hour Joe would land the helicopter.

'Where are they all?' Pa asked.

Biggles yawned, showing off his long pink tongue, then settled more deeply into the sofa.

'Anyone would think they didn't care I was going away,' Pa continued.

Biggles turned himself round in a complete circle until he was curled up like a croissant.

'Maybe they care too much,' growled a deep voice. 'Either that, or they're fed up with you going off all the time as if you didn't have a family to look after.'

'Gramps!' said Pa as his father ('Grandpa' to Oliver, Titch and Lottie) came in, lifted Biggles up and sat him on his lap. Biggles did one more turnaround as if life was one long interruption to getting comfy, and settled down.

'I suppose you've got another goodbye speech and another list of rules,' Grandpa said.

'Well . . .' said Pa, running his fingers through his straggly hair and blushing a little. 'I did think they might like to hear . . .'

'A scientific lecture,' finished Grandpa.

Pa looked anxiously towards the door, willing the others to turn up. Grandpa was the only one who could boss him about – apart, perhaps, from the Lord High Chancellor of the University of Aberdeen, but even then, of late the Chancellor had been all smiles and pats on the back.

'I promise I won't be too long this time,' he said.

'Hah!' said Grandpa. But there was no time for him to say more because the rest of the family were drifting in.

Pa considered saying, 'And what time d'you think this is?' but thought better of it. Best not to leave on a cross note. Even so, why couldn't they, well, *worship* him just a little? He thought of the university students who gazed up at him adoringly, and for a moment wished he could swap them for his family, who – much as he loved them – insisted on having minds of their own.

Ma, settling her comfy self into one of the sofas, opened her book.

'Perhaps you could leave that until later,' Pa suggested.

'But I'm just in the middle of Chapter . . .' began Ma, and then closed the book. 'Well, all right, Dear Heart. If it will make you feel better.'

'I'm perfectly well,' snapped Pa.

'The thing is,' said Ma, 'I'd rather forget you

were going off again, because I know what will happen.'

'What?' asked Titch, who was sitting on a cushion at Ma's feet, shining a piece of blue sea-glass with his hankie.

'Well, I'll cry,' said Ma, beginning to do so. 'But if I concentrate on a story, I'll be OK.'

'I really can't help it,' said Pa, beginning to feel even worse than when Grandpa had ticked him off. 'I must do this work. It's good work. It's work that will help people. Lots of people.'

'But maybe not us,' said Lottie, who had appeared when no one was looking. She was dressed in what looked like a sack with bare feet and a tatty ribbon in her hair.

'It might well be you, should you be ill,' answered Pa irritably. 'But why are you dressed like that?'

'I'm practising being an orphan,' said Lottie. 'Just in case Ma should go away too.'

'Dear Thing,' said Ma. 'I'm not going anywhere.'

'Unlike some people,' said Grandpa.

'Where's Oliver?' asked Pa. Really, this was becoming very painful! Why couldn't they just wave him off cheerfully? Wish him luck, even? They were all woe and lament. Lament and woe. Oliver was the oldest. He should set an example.

'Olly's cooking,' said Lottie. 'Cooking's comforting.'

'Go and get him,' said Pa.

'It's all right, I'm here,' said Oliver. His ginger hair was dusted with flour. He'd obviously wiped his hands on his trousers.

'Plum duff,' he said in answer to the question on everyone's faces.

'Can I have the duff without the plums?' asked Titch.

'No,' said Oliver.

Pa looked at his watch and cleared his throat.

'I am very sorry,' he began, 'that my research has not yet finished. There's more to be done. Important final tests and adjustments before we can patent this much-needed antibiotic . . .'

'We need you too,' said Oliver. He tried to

19

say it loudly and boldly but there was a lump in his throat. Why had he ever imagined he'd have a stay-at-home father?

Pa decided to trim his speech, cutting out the five paragraphs about the history of antibiotics and how lately, various epidemics had proved immune to all the old ones.

'I promise that this time I won't forget the coming home date,' he said. 'I want you all to have a lovely spring and summer, and I'll be back with you by the autumn.' Pa pulled out a big calendar, flipped the pages to *September* and the 22nd, ringed in red.

'That's if you remember to look at it,' said Titch.

'Joe's coming with me this time,' said Pa. 'He'll keep me to time.'

'Time,' said Grandpa mournfully. 'I don't have much of it left.'

'You've been saying that ever since you turned eighty,' said Pa.

'And now I'm nearly ninety-three,' said Grandpa.

'We'll look after you,' said Oliver.

'Thank you, dear boy,' said Grandpa.

'Now then,' said Pa, putting a new crisp note in his voice and half listening out for the sound of Joe's helicopter. 'I want you all to look after each other. And most importantly, to stay safe. That's why you're here, remember. It's a great pity, but the research I'm doing is so valuable that we know there are people keen to get their hands on the results and to use them not for the good of mankind, but to make lots of money. *Dizzy Perch* is the safest place I could find. But I just want to remind you about the Rules.'

'Keep the funicular oiled,' said Lottie.

'Yes,' said Pa. 'And how many *dings* to call it down to the beach?

'Three,' said Titch.

'Ma to look after the housekeeping money,' said Grandpa.

'Provided you remember to leave her some,' said Oliver.

'Of course I'll remember!' said Pa.

'We almost ran out last time,' said Oliver.

'It won't happen again,' said Pa. 'Now about my study . . . ?'

'Always keep the chest locked,' said Lottie.

'Because the magic formula's inside,' said Titch.

'*Scientific* formula,' corrected Pa. 'Science is all about reason.'

'I'm past being reasonable,' said Grandpa. 'When you get to my age it's all right to be *un*reasonable.'

'And imagination,' added Pa, in case he should sound too dull for words. 'Reason and imagination working together.'

'Olly to do the cooking,' said Ma. 'That's my favourite rule.'

'Was that a rule?' asked Pa, scratching his head. 'Please don't start inventing your own rules. I'm sure other people can help Olly with the cooking. A more important rule is that Oliver is to be our ambassador in Starwater.'

'I've forgotten what an ambassador is,' said Lottie. 'Does he get to wear a special hat?'

'It means that Olly is the only person

who has contact with the locals,' said Pa. 'Which protects you all from saying something you shouldn't.'

'Like what?' asked Titch.

'Like where I've gone!' shouted Pa. 'Or what I'm doing!' He was beginning to feel exceedingly hot and bothered. He took out his hankie and wiped his forehead.

'Do you think they'd be interested?' asked Lottie curiously.

'I only ever talk to Mrs Tansley at the Post Office, and Stan on the bus, and of course Cezary,' said Oliver.

'Your friend,' said Pa. 'I think all three are safe. I've had my people check them out. But what we do know is that there are others who, my dear Lottie, are more than interested in what I'm doing and where I'm going. Dangerously interested.'

A shiver went round the room, as if the sun had clouded over. Ma pulled a rug around her. Biggles decided he'd be better off upstairs and slid out of the door. Lottie went to sit by Oliver.

'So what is the most important rule of all?' asked Pa.

'No strangers,' said Titch.

'Apart from Grandpa's ghosts,' said Lottie.

'But they aren't strangers!' protested Grandpa.

'A lot of birds pop in,' said Titch. 'They sit on Grandpa's balcony.'

'I think they like it when I play my fiddle,' said Grandpa.

My family are entirely bonkers, thought Pa, who never knew when he was being teased. He heaved a sigh. 'Neither birds nor ghosts can be called strangers,' he said.

'Actually, birds are very strange when you think about it,' said Lottie. 'Living in the sky has to be very strange. Are there scientists investigating that?'

'Very possibly,' said Pa. 'But I'm talking about *people* who are strangers. People who ask questions . . .'

'And look suspicious,' said Titch.

'Well, they might look perfectly ordinary,' said Pa.

'And that's when they're most dangerous,' said Lottie. 'We will all need to be detectives.'

Over on her sofa, Ma had begun to weep.

'There's no need,' she said. 'No one ever visits us. Just lately I've been thinking how nice it would be if we had a visitor. Maybe someone famous . . .'

'Someone famous!' exclaimed Pa. (*What, more famous than me?* he was thinking). 'Why on earth would you want someone famous?'

'Maybe a writer,' suggested Ma, meekly. 'You know, someone who's written a lot of books.'

'Forget it, sweetie,' said Pa, crossing the room to kiss the top of her head. 'Just you carry on reading your books and forget about whoever it is that's written them.'

From outside he could hear the whoosh of Joe's helicopter growing nearer and nearer. 'Now, who's coming to wave me off?'

'Dear Heart,' said Ma, putting her book down and coming over to him. 'Hold me to your bosom and tell me you love me. Let us say our fond farewells here. I don't want to see you flying away in the sky.'

'Yuk!' said Titch.

'Like a strange bird,' said Lottie.

And then it was time for Pa to shed a tear or two because his heart was in two places – his science laboratory and his home in *Dizzy Perch* – so that it felt as if there was a tug of love in his chest. His tears surprised them all. Then Pa brushed them away, got down from his stool, hugged Ma to him and whispered something in her ear which seemed to please her.

'Maybe I'll wave to you from my tower,' said Lottie. 'I'm not keen on goodbyes.'

'Nor am I,' said Titch.

Grandpa got shakily to his feet. He too had to wipe his eyes.

'I'll not watch you go,' he said. 'But I give you my blessing!'

So it was left to Oliver to go down on the funicular with Pa, Pa with the box of groceries and the case of scientific equipment on his knee and Oliver with the big holdall.

Down on the beach Joe had kept the

helicopter's rotor blades whirling. Pa and Oliver had to duck beneath them to stow the bags. Joe opened the pilot's window to shout above the propellers' noise.

'I'll look after him!' he called to Oliver. 'But you know where to find him.'

'In an emergency,' said Pa.

'In an emergency,' echoed Oliver.

If your heart really hurt and there was an awful empty feeling in your tummy, was that an emergency? he wondered.

Pa put his hand on Oliver's shoulder. 'When it comes to looking after people while I'm away, you're the man of the family, Olly. Look after everyone at home, please – your brother and sister, and particularly your mother.'

'What about Grandpa?' Oliver asked.

Pa gave his big hearty laugh. 'Oh yes, Grandpa thinks he's looking after you, but I think you can do a bit of looking after him too. OK?'

Oliver couldn't manage a laugh. He attempted a grin that meant *Yes*, gave a big hug to Pa and, as best he could, a cheery salute to Joe. Then he stood back to watch the helicopter lift off, taking his happiness with it. He watched until the helicopter was just a speck in the sky. *Like a hummingbird*, he thought. Or maybe like a swallow following the sun to another country. Science country.

Up at the house, Ma hurried back to her room of books. *The thing is*, she said to herself, *when I've read a lot of books by one author – say, A.C. Hennessy – then I really feel I know that person. He isn't a stranger at all, so it would be quite all right to invite him to stay. It wouldn't be breaking any rules at all. I just didn't have time to explain that to Pa, but of course he would understand.*

Then Ma picked up her book again, settled herself among her rugs and shawls, and found a half-eaten doughnut to cheer herself up.

Chapter 3

Watching

Oliver watched until the sky was so empty you might have only imagined a helicopter. Then he took his solo seat on the funicular and rode up to *Dizzy Perch*.

Without Pa the house felt horribly silent. Ma, Grandpa, Lottie, Titch – not one of them was about. They'd all taken to their rooms, like rabbits to their burrows.

You didn't really realise, Oliver thought, standing in the hall and listening to the silence that was really absence, what a large and noisy person Pa was until he wasn't there. And then you remembered his laugh or how he'd shout up the stairs to bring Titch or Lottie down, or how he'd sing in the shower. (Badly. But loudly.) Oliver felt ever so slightly tearful. And as if to match his mood he heard Grandpa beginning to play his fiddle. Not one of his jolly sea-shanty tunes, more like a lament.

This won't do, Oliver told himself, drifting into Pa's study and sitting in the twirly chair at Pa's desk and doing a few twirls. Pa was relying on him, Oliver, his oldest son to look after everyone.

The study was a mess. Books scattered on the floor, mixed up with socks, T-shirts, an inside-out jersey – Pa seemed to use this room as a dressing room as much as a study. The chest was locked of course. The chest was where Pa kept a record of all his research and where, last time, Oliver had found the map that had helped him find Pa, when Pa had forgotten to come home.

Oliver put the books back on the shelf, arranged a pad of paper on the desk, and lined up several pens and pencils. Maybe having everything ready for Pa's return would make him come home sooner. It was worth a try. But, oh how he wished he could have gone with him in the helicopter! They could have squeezed him in, he thought. And he'd be just as helpful as Joe. What was it Pa had once written in a letter to Joe? *I think my eldest boy has inherited my kind of imaginative curiosity.*

There! Surely that's what Pa needed – an assistant. Imaginative curiosity.

Sitting on the floor in Pa's study, Oliver shut his eyes and pictured the log cabin in the far highlands of Scotland that was Pa's laboratory, and which no one – apart from him and Joe – had ever visited. How exciting it had been! Oliver remembered the long journey on Stan's bus from Starwater to Auchterlaldy, the steep climb up to the cabin and then bursting in on Pa, happy and angry all at once to have found him. Straight away his eyes had taken everything in – the friendliness of the wood-burning stove, the make-do book shelf, the big trestle table which later Pa had cleared of mugs and magazines so they could eat scrambled eggs together, the long bench at the back of the cabin where racks of test tubes glowed with colours and where machines with dials and lights flashed and trembled as if working on some very difficult sums.

And perhaps what had been most unexpected was that it had felt not only exciting but homely, as if this place, more than *Dizzy Perch*, was really Pa's true home. Oliver didn't want to remember that feeling. Better just to remember him and Pa sitting at the trestle table eating the best scrambled eggs ever.

The thought of the scrambled eggs made him realise it was not far off lunchtime and he hadn't done any looking after of anyone yet. He picked up Pa's favourite T-shirt. For a moment he held it to his face and sniffed Pa's smell. But that made him tearful again, so he folded it up quickly, and stashed it – along with two pairs of socks and the jersey – in the chest of drawers behind the desk. Then he closed the study door behind him, ran his fingers through his hair, straightened his shoulders, and headed for Ma's room.

Dizzy Perch was a tall, narrow house with a spiral staircase running from top to bottom. Ma and Grandpa each had a room on the second floor. Titch and Oliver were on the third and Lottie was right at the top in the lopsided tower. Oliver paused to listen at Grandpa's door. The lament had stopped. Snoring had taken over. Oliver grinned. Grandpa was probably happy with his ghosts, but Ma was probably feeling very lonely. She was probably reading and crying. Maybe he could suggest they make a shopping list together. That might distract them both from missing Pa.

He was about to knock, as he usually did – three knocks, meaning 'It's me, Oliver' – when he heard her voice chatting away as if – surely impossible – she was talking to someone. Oliver hesitated. Curiosity made him stop and listen. Either Ma was talking to herself, he decided, or, more likely, she was reading aloud. And either it was a very odd conversation or a very odd book.

'Hennessy,' said Ma. '*The Star-Crossed Lovers. Emily's Quest for Love. The Adventure in the Outback. Jenny Penny Finds a Way. Searching for Sandy. Beginning to*—'

Oliver knocked three times.

'Not now, Dear Thing,' said Ma. 'Just a little busy. Perhaps after lunch. Or maybe supper.'

'Are you all right?' Oliver asked. He was wondering if missing someone, missing Pa, had turned Ma's brains.

'I'm fine, Dear Thing,' said Ma. 'Off you pop now. No need to worry about me.'

That was all very well, thought Oliver, but who were all the people Ma was talking about – Hennessy? Emily? Jenny Penny? Sandy? He went up to his own room. Maybe if he had a little lie down before lunch he'd find an answer. Maybe if a person was lonely they began growing ghosts as friends, like Grandpa did.

He was about to drop off for forty winks when he heard it. The ding and clang-clang-clang of the funicular. Oliver knew every crank and clink of the funicular, for who oiled it once a week? So he knew it was going down. But who had called it?

Lottie? Titch? Good Lord, this looking-after business was already proving really difficult. He very much hoped Ma hadn't forgotten Pa's most important rule – NO STRANGERS. Strangers, Pa had said, were too risky. They were likely to ask too many questions, and without meaning to, one of the Coggins might talk about Pa's secret research.

By the time Oliver got downstairs, rushed to the door and looked out, the person on the funicular was off and away, hurrying along the beach, wrapped in a cape and shawl. Ma!

'But she never goes out!' Oliver said out loud because he was so surprised. What should he do? Run after her? By the time he'd hauled on the lever that brought the funicular back up, she was out of sight. Oliver tried to calm himself down. His palms were sweating and his breathing had gone all jerky like it did when he had an asthma attack. *After all*, he told himself, *be sensible, surely the only place she could go to was Starwater.* Unless she'd lost the plot, of course. Gone doolally. Maybe Pa going off again was just too much for her. She might wander on and on, looking for him. Ma didn't really know about the tides. She might drown. She might never come back. And if Pa forgot to come home again then he and Lottie and Titch wouldn't need to pretend to be orphans, they'd *be* orphans!

Panic took over. Oliver took the stairs two at a time until he was at Grandpa's room. He didn't even bother knocking on the door – which Grandpa always insisted on as being good manners – he just flung the door open, skidded on a rug, knocked over a wooden model of a unicorn, tripped over the stool on which Grandpa (snoozing in his favourite leather armchair) was resting his legs, and landed at Grandpa's large slippered feet. For a moment the room – with all Grandpa's many photographs on the walls – seemed to spin about him.

'Jings!' cried Grandpa, sitting up as upright as his old bones would allow, and with the result that Biggles, who had been very comfy in Grandpa's lap, was rudely woken up and slunk crossly away. 'Snakes and ladders, mad as hatters! What's going on? Oliver? Is that you?' cried Grandpa.

'Yes! No! Yes! It is me, but it's Ma!' panted Oliver.

'It is you? It isn't you? Just catch your breath, boy. Pass me my specs and tell me what's the matter.' Alarm made Grandpa's shaggy eyebrows shoot upwards and almost disappear into his great thatch of white hair.

Oliver searched until he'd found Grandpa's little silvery specs, which were where they usually were – under the bed.

Grandpa put them on and patted Oliver's head. 'Ah! So you're really here,' he said. 'I thought for a minute I might have been dreaming you.'

'I am here,' said Oliver, 'but Ma's not. She's gone!'

'Gone?' echoed Grandpa. 'What d'you mean, *gone*?'

'Possibly gone potty!' said Oliver. 'But I mean *gone* gone. She was in her room talking to herself and the next thing she was going down in the funicular and I saw her all hidden in a cape, hurrying along the beach like she had something . . . something really urgent to do.'

'Like post a letter?' suggested Grandpa, ruffling Oliver's hair and beginning to laugh.

'*Post a letter*?' echoed Oliver. 'But she never goes out. And she doesn't write. Well, I suppose she *can* write, but she doesn't, she reads. Anyway, who would she write to?'

'Your pa?' suggested Grandpa, putting the wooden unicorn to rights, and taking Biggles back in his lap.

'No,' said Oliver. 'Pa said no letters because that might mean someone would be able to trace him. If there is a really serious message of any sort, I'm to take it myself.'

'Of course, you're right,' said Grandpa. 'Well then, I don't know who she was writing to. I just know that she was writing to someone, because I knocked on her door to ask her if she would like to listen to my latest tune and she told me she was "Too busy, Dear Thing, writing a letter". And then she said I was to forget that, she was just doodling. But she might pop out later to post it.'

'Didn't that make you suspicious?' asked Oliver. 'Telling you she was writing a letter, and then to forget it, but she might pop out to post it?'

'I suppose you're right,' said Grandpa. 'I was just a bit fuzzled today.'

'You mean muddled,' said Oliver.

'Yes, that's it. Muddled,' said Grandpa. 'Sorry.'

'That's all right,' said Oliver grandly. 'But why didn't Ma ask me to post her letter, if she'd written one, that is? I'm the only one who goes to Starwater. I'm the one who does all the shopping . . .'

'Our ambassador,' said Grandpa.

Oliver preened a little.

'And the one who does all the cooking and cleaning,' added Grandpa. 'You're a good lad,

Oliver. But I don't know why Ma didn't give you the letter. Maybe she was feeling a bit cooped up.'

'It's never bothered her before,' said Oliver crossly. 'She likes being cooped up.'

'A bit like a mother hen,' said Grandpa, and that made them both laugh. 'Well,' Grandpa continued, 'you can watch from my balcony, if you like, to see her coming home. If you bring me some milk I'll make us some hot chocolate.'

So Oliver fetched a jug of milk and Grandpa made hot chocolate on his little primus stove, and added a plate of ginger biscuits which, he said, would keep them going until lunch, as lunch was obviously going to be late if they were waiting for Ma.

So they sat together on Grandpa's balcony (looking out to where the tide was rolled back against the sky and the sky itself was shifting colours, as if it couldn't quite decide what sort of day it was going to be), drinking hot chocolate, and eating ginger biscuits.

They sat there until they saw the small

plump bundle that was obviously Ma come scurrying back along the sand, and then they heard the *ding, clang-clang-clang* of the funicular coming up to the house.

'Maybe I should tick her off,' said Oliver, but he was too relieved that the watching was over and Ma was safely home to stop the grin spreading over his face.

'Maybe you should,' said Grandpa, grinning back at him.

Oliver wasn't the only one who'd spent the best part of the morning watching. The loud purr of the helicopter had made Big Mac rush for his telescope and shout for Moll.

'He's off!' he shouted. 'The Sworn Enemy is on the move. It's happening! Moll! Moll!

'We've got to be on our toes!

'Get one step ahead!

'Keep our eyes peeled!

'Keep a sharp look out!

'Be on the alert!

'Keep our wits about us!'

Moll, taking Amber round the field in a nice gentle trot, so that her white-stockinged hooves lifted up as elegantly as a dancer's and her high tail had the prettiest flounce, reined in beside her wild-eyed brother.

'D'you know, I just don't think we can do all that at once,' she said.

'What? What?' cried Big Mac. 'Did you see the helicopter. D'you know what that means?'

'I think you're going to tell me,' said Moll.

'It means that either he—'

'Sworn Enemy?'

'Yes, Sworn Enemy. Either he's off to wherever he's off to, to complete the sale of his research to the highest bidder—'

'Why would he do that?' asked Moll, dismounting neatly and letting Amber amble round the field by herself.

'Why would he not?' asked Big Mac. 'It could be worth a fortune.'

'Maybe he'll give it away,' suggested Moll.

'Don't be silly,' said Big Mac. (She was at it again. Mocking him).

42

'Anyway, as we don't know where he's going, there's not much we can do about it,' said Moll, 'even if we keep our eyes peeled and our ears to the ground or . . .'

By now Big Mac was jumping up and down, and the caravan was rocking on its hunkers. 'This is what we've been waiting for,' he said. 'The occupants being left alone in *Dizzy Perch*. Poor little dears! At least one of them will know exactly where Sworn Enemy has gone. And I fancy he may have left a duplicate of his research behind. All we've got to do is find a way into *Dizzy Perch*.'

'Oh easy peasy! Nothing to it,' said Moll. 'We'll just hitch a lift on that funicular railway, shall we? Then knock on the door. Say "Hello, we've come to steal your father's work. How about a cup of tea?" "Do come in," they'll say. "Welcome!" Amber needs her oats, I'm off. You can keep your wits about you.'

'Wait,' said Big Mac, grabbing her arm. 'You think I'm stupid, don't you? Well, come and look at this.' He pulled Moll into the caravan and made her sit down at the telescope. 'Now what d'you see?'

'I can't see the helicopter,' said Moll.

'Of course you can't,' said Big Mac. 'It's far, far away now. Look down. Look along the beach. Who d'you see heading for Starwater?'

'A little round person,' said Moll. 'And it's not the boy, not Sworn Enemy's oldest.'

'No,' said Big Mac. 'And does anyone else come from *Dizzy Perch* to Starwater? Have you ever seen anyone else?'

'No,' said Moll. 'And whoever it is looks anxious. He or she keeps looking over their shoulder. And is very slow. Doesn't seem very sure of the way, perhaps.'

'Is it not a sweet, little, round dumpling of a person?' cooed Big Mac.

'*A sweet, little, round dumpling* . . . ?' repeated Moll. 'Goodness me! It can't be, can it? Oh, she's coming nearer now. Beginning to hurry. Still looking behind her as if someone might be following her . . . Is it? Is it . . . ?'

'Maisie!' cried Big Mac. 'My first love. My

true love.'

'Your only love,' said Moll. 'How old were you? Twelve?'

Big Mac ignored the jibe. 'Stolen from me by Sworn Enemy,' he said. 'What does she seem to be doing?'

'It looks as if she's heading for the Post Office Stores,' said Moll.

'Let me see,' said Big Mac.

They took it in turns to watch Ma walk up and down in front of the Post Office Stores. She had borrowed Grandpa's cape which was far too big for her. Its hood kept slipping off and she kept pulling it back on so that it hid her face.

'She's got a letter in her hand,' said Big Mac.

'She's not going into the Stores,' said Moll.

'No one but the boy goes into the Stores,' said Big Mac.

'There's a letterbox in the wall,' said Moll. 'Will she? Won't she?'

'Now why would she come down here by herself?' asked Big Mac. 'She could have given the letter to the boy, but she didn't. Here she is, my sweet little dumpling, my Maisie maid . . .'

'Hardly a maid any more,' said Moll.

'She looks as if she's talking to herself,' said Big Mac.

'She looks scared,' said Moll. 'As if she doesn't know what to do.'

'There!' said Big Mac. 'She's gone and done it! She's posted it!'

'And she's off,' said Moll. 'Look, she's really in a hurry now.'

Despite herself, Moll was curious. 'What d'you think her letter was about? And who was it to?'

'Ah!' said Big Mac. 'I was waiting for you to ask.'

'D'you know?' asked Moll.

'No,' said Big Mac. 'That's for you to find out.'

'Me? How am I to do it?'

Big Mac went and sat down on the caravan's one and only seat, and put his feet up on the table. 'You're to work it out,' he said. 'Finding the answer could be our way into *Dizzy Perch*. And *that* could lead us to Sworn Enemy.'

'Short of fishing the letter out of the letterbox, I've no idea how to do it,' said Moll. 'It's impossible!'

'But it is possible that Amber might get very, very hungry,' warned Big Mac.

'You're so very, very nasty,' said Moll.

'I know,' said Big Mac, and grinned his nastiest grin.

'Dear Thing,' said Ma, when Oliver demanded to know why she'd gone out and who she was writing a letter to, if indeed she had been writing a letter. 'I've just been planning a little surprise for everyone. Maybe. If it happens, that is.'

'If what happens?' asked Oliver.

'Well, it wouldn't be a surprise if I told you, would it?' said Ma. 'Dear Thing, would you like a nice big hug?'

'Not today thank you,' said Oliver stiffly.

Chapter 4

Luck and a Letter

For over a week Moll had been racking her brains, racing Amber along the beach on the other side of Starwater, away from *Dizzy Perch*, for she didn't want to be seen by any watching Coggin until she had thought up a plan of action.

It was a sunny spring morning. Big Mac lolled lazily in a deck chair, eating peanuts and drinking cans of pop. 'You'll think of something,' he told Moll. 'A clever girl like you. How's Amber's sack of oats? Half full, is it? Or a little less?'

'Fine, so far!' snapped Moll.

She spent more time than ever grooming Amber in her stable, talking to the horse in the soft, crooning voice that made Big Mac mad. Of course he wasn't jealous of a horse, not him! Not Big Mac. Even so, whenever he heard Moll being lovey-dovey (as he put it) with Amber, he stomped back into the caravan and put the radio on very loud.

Moll didn't care. Often she sat on a stool, resting her cheek against Amber's soft chestnut flank and whispering, 'Don't worry. I won't let him harm you.' (*Or sell you*, she was thinking.) Often she stroked the white blaze on Amber's nose and told her how beautiful she was. Which was true. Then she would reach for the sugar lump in her pocket and hold it under Amber's soft muzzle. Amber replied with her idea of a kiss – which was rather lippy and sticky, but nice for all that.

But Amber needed much more than sugar lumps. Keeping a horse was probably as expensive as having a child, Moll thought. Amber needed annual injections. Her teeth had to be checked by a vet. A farrier was needed to give her new shoes. All of it cost money – money which Big Mac supplied from the money he'd inherited from their father.

It was a great pity that Big Mac had been the apple of their father's eye. Mr Malone Senior had made a lot of money selling drawing pins, and had left it all to his beloved son. Moll was given Amber, with the message: *A creature to love is of greater value than money.*

Which was true, thought Moll, *though a little looking-after money would have been very helpful.* Since he'd inherited his father's drawing-pin money, her brother hadn't done a day's work – unless you could call plotting revenge on his Sworn Enemy 'work'.

'When the drawing-pin money runs out,' said Big Mac, 'Clever-Clogs Coggin will provide!' and he roared with laughter.

'You plan to profit from your Sworn Enemy's genius and hard work, do you?' asked Moll. 'You're impossible,' she said, not for the last time.

'Just you get on with finding your way into *Dizzy Perch*,' growled Big Mac. 'Why don't you try the Post Office Stores?'

And without at all meaning to help his sister, Big Mac found he had.

'The Post Office Stores?' said Moll. 'Why would that help me get into *Dizzy Perch*?'

'Well, it might or it might not,' said Big Mac, 'but I don't see you trying anything else. Talk to the woman who runs the place. Mrs Fancy or Nancy – she knows everyone and everything in Starwater. Ask her if she's seen Maisie recently. Pretend you're a Coggin aunt or something. Just try and be useful, will you?'

'I'll do it,' Moll told Amber. 'It will keep him quiet for a bit longer. Keep us in oats.' Amber snorted an agreement. 'I don't suppose the woman in the Post Office Stores will be any help at all.'

Moll was wrong.

Mrs Emma Tansley, who ran both the Stores and the Post Office – wearing a rather dashing hat for the latter – was having a very quiet day. The postman, Mr Reginald Strut, had come in his bright red van, collected the letters from the box outside the Stores and put them in his sack ready to take to the main sorting office in town. As usual he threw the sack into the van and stopped to have a cup of tea, and maybe a cake, with Mrs Tansley.

He laid one long pink envelope on the counter in front of her.

'I don't think this one's going anywhere,' he said. 'No proper address. It'll have to be Return to Sender.'

'There may be no address on the front,' said Mrs Tansley, 'but I happen to know exactly who put this letter in the box.'

It was at this point that Moll appeared.

Knowing everyone and everything in Starwater was all well and good, Mrs Tansley often thought, *but the occasional newcomer or stranger was very welcome*. And this one, a young woman with a mane of golden hair and a look that suggested both fun and charm, brightened the morning. Mrs Tansley put on her postmistress hat to give herself a little authority.

The long pink envelope lay right in front of Moll. ('You couldn't miss it,' she told Big Mac later.) Whoever had written the letter had drawn stars all along the top and flowers all along the bottom.

'Why,' said Moll, 'that's the prettiest envelope I've ever seen!'

(Mrs Tansley didn't take her postmistress role lightly. She and Mr Strut often had a conversation about the importance of letters.

'Letters,' Mr Strut would say, 'do a lot of good deeds.'

'And are lovely,' Mrs Tansley would reply. 'The surprise of them.'

'The guess-whoness,' Mr Strut would agree.)

Mrs Tansley laid her hand on the long pink envelope and gave her new customer her best smile.

'It is indeed a very pretty envelope,' she said. 'So it's a shame it's going nowhere.'

'No proper address,' said Mr Strut rather severely.

Mrs Tansley turned the letter to face Moll.

To A.C. Hennessy
Famous author

Moll read.

'What are you going to do?' asked Moll. 'It would be such a shame for the letter not to be delivered.'

'Fortunately,' said Mrs Tansley, 'I know who's written it.'

She leant across the counter. 'You may have seen that house up high on the cliffs . . .' she began, 'it's called *Dizzy Perch*.'

Moll pricked up her ears.

'Well,' continued Mrs Tansley confidentially, 'the family who live up there . . .'

Moll seized her moment. 'Oh yes,' she said brightly, 'the Coggin family. I'm a distant relation . . .'

'You are?' said Mrs Tansley. 'Well forgive me saying so, as you're a relative, but I've always thought them a strange family, hidden up there like that. Like birds nesting on the crags, is what I sometimes say. And then none of them coming down to Starwater – except for the boy, that is. Oliver. You'll know Oliver, you being a distant relative – a nice lad. They send him down for the shopping.'

'But this letter . . . ?' prompted Moll.

'Oh yes, this letter,' said Mrs Tansley. 'I so happened to observe – not that I was watching out of course . . .'

'Of course not,' said Moll.

'When I saw her,' said Mrs Tansley.

'"Her"?' said Moll and Mr Strut together.

'The boy's mother. Oliver's mother. All hidden in a cloak and looking over her shoulder as if she didn't want to be seen, and not coming *in* to the Post Office like she might have done, popping in to say hello or something. No. Just slips the letter into the box outside and hurries off. Now, you can see she hasn't even bothered with a stamp! Thinks stars and flowers will do it.'

'She's a recluse,' said Mr Strut. 'That's what I think. All of them. Recluses.'

'Except Oliver,' said Mrs Tansley loyally.

'But as you're a distant relative . . . How distant would that be?'

'Second cousin twice removed,' Moll improvised.

'Well, then, perhaps you're going to visit,' suggested Mrs Tansley, 'and you could take this letter with you, and ask Mrs Coggin to put an address on it?'

'And a stamp,' said Mr Strut.

'Well, of course I could,' said Moll, picking up the letter and sliding it into her pocket before Mrs Tansley could have second thoughts.

'Much appreciated,' said Mrs Tansley. 'Are you staying locally? I hope we may see you again?'

But the only answer was the bell of the door closing and her new and charming customer almost running away.

'Well!' said Mr Strut.

'Well!' said Mrs Tansley. 'Second cousin twice removed or not – she's certainly one of those Coggins. Odd!'

* * *

'What's this?' asked Big Mac, when Moll laid the letter in front of him.

'I think it's what you want,' said Moll. 'A way in to *Dizzy Perch*. It's from your sweetie pie, your beloved, your one and only Maisie Coggin.'

'Stop your mocking,' growled Big Mac, slitting the letter open with a kitchen knife. 'How did you get this?'

'I told the postmistress I was a second cousin twice removed. I hope it was only a very small lie.'

Big Mac gave a hoot of laughter. 'Second cousin twice removed? Very good! I like it. Now what does this say?'

The letter, on matching pink paper, was decorated with more stars and flowers. Big Mac spread it flat on the table. Moll perched on a stool.

Dear A.C. Hennessy, Big Mac read.

I am a great fan. Maybe your greatest fan. I have read lots and lots of your books and loved them all. The ones I like best are:

The Star-Crossed Lovers
Emily's Quest for Love
Adventure in the Outback
Jenny Penny Finds a Way
Searching for Sandy
Beginning to Know Love

I'm writing to ask if you would like to come and stay with me (and my family) in our house near the village of Starwater. Our house, Dizzy Perch, is set high up on the cliffs above the sea. I think the house might give you lots of inspiration for one of your wonderful stories. I can promise that you would get all the peace and quiet you need. My son, Oliver, is a very good cook and we have a spare study where you could work.

To get here you need to come to Starwater and then look east to see Dizzy Perch. Wait for the tide to be out, then walk along the beach. We have a funicular railway, so if you ring the bell at the bottom, it will be sent down to fetch you.

I do hope you will do me, your greatest fan, the honour of a visit.

Yours very hopefully,
Maisie Coggin xxx

'Why on earth does she put kisses?' asked Big Mac crossly.

'It doesn't matter!' said Moll. 'Now you've got your way in. There's no address on this letter. Mrs Tansley says it needs an address and a stamp. You can do a good deed and take it back to Maisie. No doubt she'll take one look at you and say "Mac, darling come in, come in!" And then you can ask her, very nicely, where Sworn Enemy has gone.'

'Are you off your head?' asked Big Mac. 'Of course she won't ask me in! The poor woman is still foolishly in love with him, the horrible Amos. She knows perfectly well I'm his rival. There's no way I can show myself until I can show *her* that I'm the better man. No, sister dear, it's *you* who are going to visit *Dizzy Perch*.'

'Me? I suppose you want me to pretend I'm that second cousin twice removed?'

'No, no, no!' said Big Mac shaking his head. 'You're so short of imagination. You're to be A.C. Hennessy.'

Chapter 5

Who Goes There?

It was Lottie, up in her tower, who saw them first – Moll and Amber, racing along the beach beneath *Dizzy Perch*, Moll's wild mane of golden hair streaming behind her, Amber's chestnut coat glowing in the morning sun.

'Oh!' said Lottie, 'Oh! Oh! Oh!' and she leant so far out of the window, she almost fell out.

It happened to be one of those days when Lottie had been daydreaming she was really the daughter of a rich and beautiful princess and that one day her real mother would appear. Lottie enjoyed pretending this and thinking how surprised everyone would be when it was discovered she too was a princess.

So when she saw Moll – Moll who, indeed, was looking very beautiful that morning – it was as if the mother-princess of her daydream had arrived. Lottie felt as gooey as chocolate cream, with delight.

She wasn't the only one to see Moll and Amber.

Titch was sitting on the big flat stone at the top of the funicular railway, arranging his latest pieces of sea glass in a pattern.

Moll, trying to get up her courage to ding the bell of the funicular, galloped up and down, and up and down. It was the sound of Amber's hooves which made Titch look up, and when he did, several pieces of sea glass went clattering down the side of the cliff.

It wasn't Moll who caught Titch's eye. Why would anyone bother about a woman with straggly gold hair, wearing jeans and an old blue jersey when there, beneath him on the beach was the most wonderful creature he'd ever seen! This high-stepping chestnut horse with a white blaze on her nose, white stockinged legs, and a tail that was a pure lilt of loveliness.

'Like a flame!' Titch whispered to himself. And there was a feeling in his heart he had never felt before. 'Awesome!' said Titch. 'If only,' said Titch, and he didn't know what his *if only* meant, except his hands ached to stroke the chestnut coat of this beautiful creature, to sit on its back, to gallop along the beach fast as the wind.

Apart from Lottie and Titch, there was one other person who saw Moll and Amber. Grandpa. Grandpa was late out of bed. He'd had one of his long dreams full of his friendliest ghosts. He was feeling very happy. Without his specs and still in his nightshirt, he wandered out on to his balcony. Opening his mouth in a great yawn, he stretched his arms out by way of saying good morning to the day. Then he saw her. A combination of the sun in his eyes and the flash of Moll and Amber, of gold and chestnut, made him gasp and rub his eyes. Grandpa was, after all, ninety-two, and his mind was a little muddled. He missed his son and he missed

Grandma Coggin even more. Often he wondered if she was up in heaven looking down on him. So now, not completely awake, and dazzled by the sunshine and by the vision of Moll and Amber as they sped past in a blur of colour, Grandpa had to hold on to the low rail of his balcony to keep himself steady.

'Eureka!' Grandpa said. 'An angel! *I lifted up mine eyes, and beheld an angel of the Lord, riding one of the spirits of heaven!*' He would have fallen to his knees if his knees hadn't been far too stiff. Instead – and because he now felt fully awake – he went back into his room and fetched his specs.

Amber was panting, her flanks steaming. Moll slowed her to a trot, then reined her in and slid off her back. Fixed in one of the rocks, was an old iron hook that had been used for mooring a boat. Using the reins and a plait of rope, Moll tied Amber up.

'I've got to do it,' she whispered in the horse's velvet ear. 'I've got to get into *Dizzy Perch* and pretend I'm A.C. Hennessy. I've got to do it for you, Amber. I've got to find out where Sworn Enemy has gone.'

'Ah!' said Grandpa, back on his balcony, with a rug round his shoulders and his specs on his nose, 'not an angel after all. Well, one can hope. And it looks as if we have a visitor. Yippee!' And even with his stiff knees, Grandpa almost skipped back into his room. He just had time to pull on his old corduroy trousers with their red braces, and to get his arms into his shirt sleeves, and his head out without undoing the buttons, when he heard it. The familiar ding of the bell that called down the funicular. Only, of course Moll didn't know about three rings. How could she? But she climbed over the gate, got up her courage and dinged the bell as hard as she could. The ding rang through *Dizzy Perch* rattling the windows, shaking a fine rain of sawdust down from the roof, making everyone inside stop absolutely still and listen.

There was pandemonium. Lottie flew down the spiral staircase from her wonky tower. Titch, suddenly terrified, rushed inside, pushing the big front door shut. Both of them clutched hold of Grandpa who had plodded downstairs trying not to feel too excited.

'It's her!' said Lottie. 'She's *so* beautiful!'

'Can she bring the horse in?' asked Titch.

'Don't be ridiculous,' said Grandpa. 'Where's Oliver?'

'Here,' said Oliver coming out of the kitchen. 'Who's beautiful? And what horse?'

Again Moll pulled the bell until it gave another echoing *DIIIIIING!*

And that one brought Ma trundling out of her room. 'Dear Things!' she said. 'What's going on? Someone wants up on the funicular. Is anyone going to do anything?'

'No,' said Oliver. 'Pa said no visitors.'

'We could just say hello,' said Lottie. 'She may have come a long way.'

'She?' asked Oliver.

'The angel,' said Grandpa. 'I mean, a young woman who *looks* very like an angel.'

'And has a fabulous beast,' said Titch.

'A horse,' said Grandpa.

'Well,' said Oliver, 'seeing that you're all so keen to see her, we'll send the funicular down, and she can say hello, and then we'll tell her we don't want anything today, thank you.'

'Don't we?' asked Titch. 'Want anything today, I mean.'

Oliver sighed. 'That's what you say when someone comes to your door selling things. My friend Cezary told me. Sometimes someone comes with a suitcase full of things to sell, but if you don't want anything you just say, "No, thank you" very politely and they go away.'

'She doesn't have a suitcase,' said Lottie, her lower lip trembling.

'I suppose she might want to sell us a horse,' said Titch hopefully.

Diiiiiiiiiing went the bell again.

'Oh snakes and ladders, mad as hatters!' exclaimed Grandpa. 'We can't do anything until we find out who she is and what she wants. Lottie – send down the funicular!'

Lottie didn't need to be asked twice. She yanked open the heavy front door and leapt for the lever that sent the funicular clanging down the side of the cliff.

Amber, hearing the noise, snorted her alarm.

'What is the most important rule of all?' Oliver asked. But they'd all gone to the open door to watch the funicular coming slowly up towards them, so no one was listening when he repeated the answer, as given by Pa: 'No strangers.'

'Dear Thing,' said Ma, ruffling his hair.

The funicular was very bumpy. All the Coggins were used to it. Moll held on tightly, thinking she might be flung out at any moment. She had a small leather bag with her in which she'd put the sort of items she imagined a famous author might carry – a notepad, several pens and pencils, a pencil sharpener, a rubber and a green eyeshade for inspiration. She also had the letter in its pink envelope.

'A.C. Hennessy. A.C. Hennessy. I am A.C. Hennessy,' Moll said to herself, as the funicular clanged upwards and she saw a row of heads, three of them with tufty ginger hair, one with wild white hair, and one of grey-brown frizz staring down at her.

Then with a final *clang* she landed. And suddenly, as if she was now on stage, all Moll's memories of school plays (of which she'd been particularly fond) came back to her, and without missing a heartbeat, she took on her new character.

Moll stepped lightly off the funicular and smiled at them all.

'I'm A.C. Hennessy,' she said.

Ma swooned. That is to say she went red and then white, then a mix of both, and then she toppled backwards. Grandpa just managed to catch her. He lowered her gently to the floor.

'Who?' asked four voices.

'A.C. Hennessy,' said Moll again.

'The famous author!' said Ma. 'And I thought you were a man.'

For a moment Moll was caught off guard. Why hadn't she and Big Mac considered whether A.C. Hennessy was a man or a woman? But she was soon swept up in her new role again. She laughed. 'The initials,' she said, 'lead lots of people astray. A for Alice, C for Caroline, but otherwise known as Ace, like the Ace of Hearts.' (*Where was all this coming from?* she wondered. Maybe she really was some kind of author, only she hadn't known it before.)

'Ace of Hearts!' echoed Lottie. (*Forget 'Dear Thing'*, she was thinking, *how about 'Daughter of Ace of Hearts'?*)

'Ace!' said Titch admiringly. 'That's – well, ace! But what's your horse called?'

'Amber,' said Moll/Ace.

'Ace and Amber,' said Titch. 'Perfect.'

Ma had heaved herself up, found a chair, sat herself down and was now fanning herself with a book (*Jenny Penny Finds a Way* by you-know-who).

'Dear Things,' she began.

'Now wait a minute,' interrupted Oliver. 'Do you know this lady?' *Sly*, he was thinking, she looked very sly. 'Who is she?'

'Dear Thing, she's just told you. This is the

famous author A.C. Hennessy, and I invited her. Well, him, only it turns out he's a her.'

'You invited her!' cried Oliver.

Moll/Ace pulled the pink envelope out of her bag and waved it at him.

Oliver snatched it from her. Read it and tore it in half. He could feel the blood rushing to his head as if his brains might pop out. 'You invited her!' he repeated. 'Have you completely forgotten everything Pa said before he went away? Forgotten the most important rule of all?'

Ma wriggled uncomfortably.

'NO STRANGERS,' said Oliver, speaking in capital letters.

'But, Dear Thing, she isn't really a stranger. I've read all her books, well nearly all. I've read *The Star-Crossed Lovers, Emily's Quest for Love, Adventure in the Outback, Searching for—*'

'Never mind all that,' said Oliver. He was almost hopping with rage. Why, it wouldn't have surprised him if Titch had done something silly, something dangerous, or Lottie, or even

70

Grandpa, but Ma! *Look after everyone*, Pa had said. *Your brother and sister and particularly your mother.* And now she was the one who had broken the most important rule of all!

'Reading someone's books isn't the same as *knowing* them,' Oliver said.

Ma looked pained. 'But Dear Thing, I *feel* as if I know her.

'Your mother thought *Dizzy Perch* might give me inspiration,' said Moll/Ace, for this wasn't going at all well. The thought of going back to Big Mac and telling him she'd failed was horrendous.

'And she could put us all in a book,' added Ma.

'I don't want to be in a book,' snapped Oliver. He felt like hiding his face in case Ace was writing about him in her head. Wasn't that what authors did? He scowled at her.

What a nice boy, Moll thought. *Bright as a button. Really caring about his family and trying to do what his father's asked him to do.* And then she pushed such thoughts away. She was

71

here to find out where Oliver's father, Big Mac's Sworn Enemy, had gone. It was no good beginning to *like* one of the children.

'Well, I'm here now . . .' she began.

Ma began to sob. 'And I shall be very unhappy, Oliver, if you even think of sending her away,' she said, wiping her eyes with the edge of her shawl.

'So shall I,' piped up Lottie.

'And me,' said Titch though in a very small voice because at heart he thought Oliver was right. Ace *was* a stranger. But then you couldn't call a horse a stranger, could you? And he thought he couldn't bear it if she rode away on Amber and he never saw them again.

'I don't think anyone – not even your pa – would consider this nice young lady any kind of threat,' said Grandpa. He was thinking how pleasant it would be to show her all his photographs, and tell her about his ghosts. Indeed, he thought, he could tell her lots of stories, and she could write them all down and put them in a book. The prospect would cheer the evenings up. He would invite her into his room for hot chocolate.

'Dear Thing . . .' wheedled Ma. 'Maybe just for a little while . . . ?'

They were all lined up, looking at him. Waiting.

'Pleeeeease!' said Lottie.

'You can't call a horse a stranger,' said Titch.

'Maybe we can just make an exception for Miss Hennessy . . . ?' said Grandpa.

'Ace,' said Moll/Ace – or was she now Ace/Moll?

'Ace,' said Grandpa shyly.

Oliver shut his eyes. He tried to remember Pa's voice, to hear it in his head. He rehearsed the Rules as quickly as he chanted the times table with Grandpa – *oil the funicular, look after the housekeeping money, keep the chest locked, be the ambassador in Starwater . . .'*

He opened his eyes. They were all still waiting. They were looking at him as if it was in his power to give them something they badly, badly wanted – or to take it away. He felt as if he was being tugged in half. But how could he resist their pleading faces? He would explain it all to Pa when he got the chance. Pa knew about Ma and her books. He'd understand. Wouldn't he?

'Well,' said Oliver, 'just for a little while.'

'Dear, Dear Thing,' said Ma.

'Yippee!' said Grandpa.

Down on the beach Amber whinnied.

Chapter 6

The Ace of Hearts

What really bugged Oliver – apart from the fact that the whole family was breaking Pa's most important rule, and that he, Oliver, should have stopped them – was the fact that everyone in *Dizzy Perch* behaved as if they were under an enchantment. All of them – Ma, Grandpa, Lottie, Titch – were besotted by the Ace of Hearts.

Never had Ma seemed quite so happy. She had tidied her room and brought in an extra chair so that Ace could come and read to her from one of Ace's own books which she'd signed in red ink with a great flourish. Interrupting one of these readings to bring both of them a resentfully bitter cup of coffee, Oliver couldn't help noticing that Ace was a very poor reader and often seemed to stumble over the longer words which was odd as presumably she'd written them. Ma didn't seem to care. Unwrapping herself of her many shawls and scarves, Ma seemed to be shedding years of unhappiness as, with her eyes half closed in pleasure, she listened to Ace reading.

And then there was Lottie and Titch. Seeing Ace plaiting Lottie's hair or the pair of them making clothes for peg dolls made Oliver realise that his sister had mostly been a lonely little girl. *Perhaps we've all been lonely*, he thought. *Lonely in a way you hardly notice, until someone comes along to make you unlonely.*

Sometimes, while he was cooking supper, he could partly hear Lottie and Ace chatting together in the sitting room. Cross as he was, he liked hearing their voices – Lottie's light, Ace's deeper. Either they were having an earnest discussion about careers for girls, or it was girly stuff about hair and make up. Once his ears pricked up and he actually went to the door so he could listen in properly. That was when he heard Ace asking questions about Pa. *Sly questions*, Oliver thought.

'You must be missing your father,' she said. 'I expect you know where he is though, don't you?'

'No,' said Lottie.

'Does he write to you?' asked Ace.

'Shall we make a school for the dolls?' asked Lottie.

As for Titch, he was a different boy! Titch forgot all about his collection of pebbles and sea glass. Tap dancing, he said, was for babies. Titch had fallen in love with a horse! He was hardly ever in the house when he could be down on the beach with Amber.

At first, what to do with Amber had been a big problem. She couldn't be left on the beach all day. Every night Ace rode away, taking Amber – she said – to the stable she'd arranged for her. But where was that, Oliver wanted to know. No one seemed to know or care. As long as Amber came back in the morning, that was all that mattered.

'She's not staying long,' Oliver said every morning at breakfast.

'Dear Thing,' said Ma patting his cheek. 'Such a good boy.'

'Misery guts,' said Lottie.

'Amber is an Arab mare,' said Titch. 'She is fourteen hands high. Did you know, Oliver, that's how you measure a horse?'

'I don't want to know,' said Oliver crossly.

So that Amber had shelter during the day, Titch, Grandpa and Ace had made a rough stable in the largest of the caves on the beach. Grandpa had been only too pleased to make a wooden trough and a wooden rail with pegs for hanging bridles and reins and the rugs Amber needed when the wind was sharp. Ace herself had brought along hay and oats in two big saddlebags.

'Now we're all set up,' Grandpa said happily, surveying his handiwork.

'For the time being . . .' said Oliver.

'I can be Amber's groom,' said Titch. 'And Ace is going to teach me to ride.'

'I doubt there'll be time for that,' said Oliver.

At which point Titch burst into tears.

'Oliver,' said Grandpa, 'I wish you'd remember your manners. A guest isn't the same as a stranger. A guest must always be made welcome. Miss Hennessy' – (Grandpa hadn't yet managed to call her Ace) – 'has cheered us all up. She's like a breath of fresh air. The dear girl's a godsend!'

A godsend? thought Oliver, outraged. He was about to point out there was a difference between a guest and a stranger, in that a guest was usually someone invited. Then he remembered Ma's letter and said nothing. He'd hoped Grandpa would be on his side – for no one else seemed to be – but Grandpa had become as enchanted with Ace and Amber as everyone else. A godsend indeed!

Grandpa had been reading up about horses. Ace actually kissed him on the cheek when he gave them all a talk on the wonders of Arab horses and how the Bedouins, who were the people of the desert, gave the first Arabian horse the title *Drinker of the Wind*. And that once upon a time the angel Gabriel – (Grandpa had angels on his mind) – turned a thundercloud into the prancing, handsome creature that became the horse.

'Just a stupid story,' said Oliver, though he felt so charmed by it he almost began to like Ace.

'Stories matter,' said Grandpa.

'So does the truth,' said Oliver.

What had made him say that, he wondered afterwards. Was it because they all seemed against him? Why did he feel so uneasy whenever Ace was around?

In bed at night, Oliver had an imaginary conversation with Pa in which he said things like *If you could see how happy Ace makes everyone – particularly Ma – I think you wouldn't mind her being here*. But some corner of his mind seemed to answer back that Pa *would* mind. It was the corner of his mind that felt there was something not quite right about A.C. Hennessy, even if he couldn't put his finger on it. It was the corner of his mind that wondered why Ace, as a famous author, never seemed to do any writing. And why she asked everyone about Pa. Where was he? Did they know when he would be coming back? What exactly was he doing?

To Oliver's disgust, Ma had said that Ace could borrow Pa's study. Oliver made sure to go in every day to see if anything had been disturbed – like the chest, or the drawers of Pa's desk. But nothing had been touched. And though Ace had laid her notebook, her pens, pencils, rubbers and pencil sharpener in a neat line on Pa's desk, when Oliver had peeped into the notebook, it was empty.

He mentioned this fact to Ma. 'Ace never seems to write anything,' he said. 'Have you noticed?'

'Dear Thing,' said Ma, 'I don't suppose you can understand how writers work, how their brains are different from ours, how they have this special gift. They have imagination, Dear Boy. Big imaginations. Ace will be gathering ideas all the time she is with us, absorbing the atmosphere of the place, allowing ideas to grow like . . . like seeds that grow into flowers.'

'Well, I thought she might at least make a few notes,' said Oliver.

'It will all be in her head,' said Ma. 'Don't you worry about it.'

But Oliver did. So when Ace came into the kitchen offering help – though really, he thought, it was to ask him questions about Pa – he decided he would do the asking of questions.

'I was wondering,' said Oliver, 'where you get your ideas from?'

Ace/Moll was peeling potatoes at the sink. 'Ideas?' she said, searching her head for an answer. Where on earth *did* writers get their ideas from?

'I dream them,' she said at last. 'I dream them overnight, and I wake up and there's an idea ready for me to write it all down.'

'Sort of like plucking them out of the sky?' said Oliver.

'Exactly,' said Ace/Moll. 'I expect your father has lots of ideas, hasn't he? Maybe he writes them all down. Puts them somewhere safe.'

'I wouldn't know,' said Oliver. 'You can leave the potatoes. I'll finish peeling them.'

Reluctantly, Ace/Moll put down the knife. Of all the family, somehow she liked Oliver most. He did so much looking after. It was always Oliver who did the shopping, the cooking, and the tidying, and who seemed to care for all of them. She liked his sturdy independence, the fact he wasn't always trying to please her like the others did. In fact, what she liked most was that he didn't seem quite so taken in by A.C. Hennessy. *He doubts me*, she thought. *He's clever*. And she shivered a little, thinking of Big Mac's anger if she didn't find out where Sworn Enemy was living. The only dream Moll/Ace had was of Amber being taken away and sold to some cruel circus owner.

So far, none of them had been any help. Any

mention of Pa only made Ma cry.

'Ah, only an artist like yourself can understand,' Ma said for she liked to speak poetically when talking of Pa, 'when I tell you that my heart-bird follows wherever he goes.'

'And where might that be?' asked Moll/Ace.

'Who can tell of the flights of love?' asked Ma, dabbing her eyes with an old duster she'd found under the bed.

'Who indeed,' said Moll/Ace.

Neither Lottie nor Titch had been any help. Moll wondered if either of them missed their father at all. Maybe they were used to him going away.

'There's less trouble when Pa's away,' said Titch. 'I don't think he can ride a horse.'

'Actually,' said Lottie, 'I don't see much of him even when he *is* at home.'

Grandpa, thought Moll. Grandpa loved to talk. And there was that offer of a hot chocolate together with a look at all his photographs. *But not yet*, she thought. Oliver was already wary. Best not to arouse any suspicions just yet.

* * *

Every evening, before it was dark, Moll rode back to Big Mac and the caravan. Even Amber seemed reluctant to go, turning her head towards Titch as he came down on the funicular to give her a last carrot or piece of apple. And Amber, that *Drinker of the Wind*, usually so ready to fly along the beach, had to be given a gentle thwack on her rump to get her going. *She likes it here*, thought Moll. *And so do I.*

The caravan seemed cold and bleak compared to *Dizzy Perch. Big Mac could do with an Oliver*, she thought, looking at the sink that was full of unwashed dishes, the table with the remains of a tin of beans, the bunk bed which was strewn with unwashed clothes.

Moll gave Amber her last feed of the day, made sure her hay and her water were fresh, and kissed her goodnight.

'It's me you should be looking after,' growled Big Mac. He was sitting at the table with a map on one side and a book on the other. *Elegant*

Solutions: Ten Beautiful Experiments in Chemistry, Moll read.

'Doing your own research for a change,' she said.

'There's others on the same trail as him,' said Big Mac. 'After the same formula. That's what. We need to get to him first. So what have you found out or have you just been having a jolly at my expense?'

'It's not costing you anything,' said Moll.

'That darn horse is costing me plenty,' said Big Mac. 'I suppose it'll be the farrier next. New shoes. Or her teeth needing a polish.'

'Both,' said Moll.

'So, what have you found out?'

'Nothing,' said Moll. 'I don't think any of them really know where Sworn Enemy has gone.'

'Of course they do!' roared Big Mac. 'Maisie must know. The boy must know – the oldest boy – and the old man.'

'Well, if they do, they're not saying!'

Big Mac thumped the table, so that *Ten*

Beautiful Experiments in Chemistry went bouncing off the table.

'It's your job to *make* them say. To wheedle it out of them. And there must be papers. Research papers somewhere. A safe, even.'

'No,' said Moll. 'There isn't a safe. I'm in his study and . . .'

'You're in his study? Holy smoke, girl! There have to be papers there. Notebooks. Workings out. Geometry and algebra. Mathematical equations. Results!'

'There's a chest . . .' said Moll.

'A chest?' Big Mac's eyebrows shot to the top of his head. 'A chest? And inside . . . ?

'It's locked,' said Moll.

'My sister's an idiot,' said Big Mac. 'I don't care how you do it. I don't care if you have to find the key for it. I don't care if you have to use a hammer on it. But one way or another, get it open. And get one of them talking. It only takes one of them to spill the beans.'

'They're nice,' said Moll. 'They're all nice. Ma and Lottie and Titch and Oliver. All of them.'

'Holy Smoke and Fried Onions,' said Big Mac. 'You're not there to *like* them! Just keep it in that idiot head of yours. It's finding Sworn Enemy or goodbye Amber. Got it?'

'Got it,' said Moll.

That night she slept in the hayloft above Amber's stable. All night she heard the horse's soft snuffles. The smell of her was sweetly comforting.

Chapter 7

Biggles and the Ghosts

The first week was almost up when Oliver discovered he wasn't the only one who felt suspicious of Ace.

There was Biggles.

Whenever he saw Ace, Biggles hissed, arching his back and showing his tiny, sharp teeth. He wouldn't stay in the same room with her, slinking away as soon as she appeared.

'Be nice!' Lottie told him, but clearly Biggles didn't feel like being nice.

'Maybe it's not Ace, but Amber,' suggested Titch. 'Perhaps Biggles can smell her.'

But Ace or Amber, it didn't seem to matter. Once, when Ace tried to win Biggles over, picking him up and scratching his head between his ears – an event that usually had Biggles purring with delight – Biggles stretched out one long paw of claws and drew blood from Ace's arm.

'I think he's just jealous,' said Ma, 'and wanting attention.'

And then there were Grandpa's ghosts.

All the Coggins were used to Grandpa's ghosts. Years ago, Ma had explained how, when a person was very old, they had real friends and ghost friends. 'The ghost friends are the ones who've died, but you don't forget them and they don't forget you. They become a bit like characters in a book,' said Ma.

On dull winter nights when there was nothing better to do, the Coggins lined up on the spiral staircase, to listen to Grandpa talking to his ghosts. Sometimes it was his chum who had shared his interest in steam trains, and sometimes it was Grandma Coggin. Grandpa would talk to her in a low, tender voice, play his fiddle, and sing her a love song that made Lottie cry.

Ma had been very pleased with the notion that ghosts were like characters in a book, and in a way, now that they had a real live author living with them, so was Grandpa. And although he didn't say so at once, he was hoping to introduce Ace to one or two ghosts, who she might like to include in her next story. But neither Jim, his steam train chum, nor Grandma Coggin would speak to him.

'I don't understand it,' Grandpa said to Oliver. 'It's almost as if they've been switched off. D'you think maybe they're shy?'

'Or they don't like writers,' suggested Oliver.

Oliver had been working up his courage to tell Ma – to tell all of them – that it was time A.C. Hennessy left, and to remind them, yet again, of Pa's rule about strangers. *I'm going to upset everyone*, he thought, *I'm going to be the least popular person in* Dizzy Perch. *Me and Biggles*.

Oliver had read that animals sometimes know things people don't. *Perhaps*, he thought,

Biggles knows something's not right about Ace. And, pleased to have at least the cat on his side, he gave Biggles an extra sardine with his supper. And then, for the umpteenth time, he tried to work out what it was about Ace that made him uneasy, when clearly she made everyone else happy.

After all, wasn't it quite natural she should ask questions about Pa? You'd surely expect a father to be around at least some of the time. And maybe Ma was right, and writers had different brains from everyone else, and they didn't need to keep writing things down or making notes. They were growing Ideas in the dark of their heads, all the time. (This made Oliver think he would like to see an Idea popping out of Ace's head like a flower from a flowerpot.) And did all writers go galloping about on horses? Somehow Oliver thought not.

Perhaps the best thing he could do, he decided, would be to look at Ace's books – at least if he looked at the dust jackets they would tell him something about A.C. Hennessy, and that would prove she was real. Real? Did he think she wasn't real? Was he going out of his mind? Was he getting a Biggles-mind? Well, he would look at the books. That would settle it.

But that wasn't as easy as he thought it would be. He chose an evening, when Ace had ridden away, to take Ma a bedtime cocoa. Ma's room was much tidier than usual. True, the sewing machine was still surrounded by bales of materials. Strips of buttons and zips dangled rather dustily from hooks above a shelf of bright cottons. But the books, which of late had been stacked in towers or shoved under the bed or even *in* the bed, had now been neatly shelved. It had to be said that most of the books, to Oliver's shame, bore the mark of a library on their spine. From time to time, Oliver tried to work out the size of the library fine Ma must owe but it had become too large even to think about. But not A.C. Hennessy's books. Oliver knew perfectly well these had been bought new. Ordered (he'd written the order himself) from the bookshop in Brochmuir, and delivered – more or less one a month – to the Post Office in Starwater.

Ma was stitching pieces of patchwork together. It looked as if she'd cut up about three old blankets into squares and diamonds and hexagons and that she was now putting them together.

'A rug for Amber,' she explained, spitting out pins. 'Ace asked me.'

'What else did she ask you?' Oliver jumped in with his own question.

'Dear Thing,' said Ma, 'I know you're not happy having Ace here, but when she's written her wonderful story about us, I'm sure you will be. And so will Pa,' she added. 'So don't you be making a fuss about her staying on for a little longer.'

'I was wondering about her books,' said Oliver. 'Perhaps I could have a look?'

'Dear Thing! That's really nice of you. Of course. I've put them all in that basket because they're so special.'

Oliver found the shopping basket full of books – A.C. Hennessy's books – beside Ma's bed.

'There's no covers on them!' he exclaimed. 'They're – why, they're naked!'

'Dear Thing!' giggled Ma. 'Of course they're not naked. Ace suggested we take off the covers to keep them nice and clean. So you see, I've wrapped them in this quite pretty wallpaper and written the titles on them and, of course, Ace's name. I thought I'd done it rather nicely, don't you think? Ace was ever so pleased.'

Oliver found it hard to hide his frustration. 'So where are the covers?' he asked.

'Oh Ace is looking after them for me,' said Ma, picking up another patch and pinning it in place. 'Don't look so miserable, Dear Thing. Why don't you ask Ace if she'll write a story specially for you?'

'I'm not certain she *can* write,' said Oliver crossly.

'Now you're being really silly,' said Ma. 'Why don't you go and see that friend of yours in Starwater? Whatshisname.'

'Cezary,' said Oliver.

'That should cheer you up,' said Ma. 'Tell him all about our famous author. I expect he'll be really envious.'

Cezary! thought Oliver. *My one and only friend.* Well, there was Stan, the bus driver, who had helped him to find his Pa, and who knew how hard it was to be the oldest boy in the family. Stan was definitely a friend too, but Cezary . . . well, Cezary, who'd come all the way from Poland to Starwater, was . . . well, he was a chum. A special chum. Furthermore, Pa had said that Stan and Cezary were 'safe', which meant it was OK to talk to them. They could be trusted. But would Cezary understand? Would he, like Ma suggested, just be envious that they had a famous author staying with them – or would he understand Oliver's doubts and suspicions? *He'll listen*, Oliver said to himself. *Cezary is good at listening. And he's good at having ideas.*

* * *

Bright and early the next morning, before anyone was awake, Oliver was up and out and on his way to Starwater. He was feeling better than he'd felt all week. As if to cheer him on his way the sky was slowly lightening as though someone was pulling back the curtain of dark, and there was the sky – pink, purple and pale, pale blue. And there were all the seagulls yowling and howling as if they'd never seen a new day before.

Oliver had taken the back route over the rocks so he wouldn't wake anyone up on the clangy funicular, or meet Ace and Amber galloping along the beach towards *Dizzy Perch*. Oliver was sure-footed as a goat on these rocks. They were as familiar to him as if they were his own back path, which in a way they were. Barefoot, he leapt nimbly from rock to rock, flat or sharp, fat or thin, seaweedy or barnacled, on he went, hurrying now, running along the Creel Road that led into the village, his heart saying, *Can't wait! Can't wait!*

And there, just as he was running out of

breath, was Starwater. Oliver caught a glimpse of Mrs Tansley opening up the Post Office Stores for the morning newspapers. It was too early perhaps for Stan and his rackety old bus. But not too early for the fishermen who would have been out for a good part of the night, looking for crabs and lobsters. Oliver searched the harbour for their boats, and for one boat in particular. Two of them, *Magnet* and *Exuberant* were still out, though he could see *Exuberant* heading for the harbour, fluffing up a wake behind it. *Magnet* was a tiny dot in the distance, haloed by a crowd of gulls.

But hurray, hurray! There, anchored in the harbour, was *Nadzieja* – the word meant 'Hope' in Polish – the boat that belonged to Cezary's father. And there was Cezary himself, running down to help his father with the nets, his black and white dog, Cheerio, at his heels. Cezary stopped in his tracks when he saw Oliver, waved furiously and beckoned him down to the harbour. The boys punched each other's arms by way of *Hello, happy to see you.*

Cezary's father was taking off his oilskins, and spreading his nets out on the harbour's quayside.

'I'm done for the day, boys,' he said. 'You two can go swap secrets together. I expect there'll be a hot drink for you too. Maybe even breakfast for you, Olly.'

'How d'you know we have secrets?' asked Oliver, feeling slightly alarmed.

Cezary's father laughed and shook some water at him from his sou'wester.

'Don't boys always have secrets?' he asked.

'Maybe,' laughed Oliver. Just being with Cezary and his father made him feel comforted.

The boys raced up the road, past the Post Office Stores and up to Seaview Terrace, the six fishermen's cottages, each with a tidy garden that looked down on the village. Cezary's house was Number 3. Compared to *Dizzy Perch*, it was as small as a doll's house. Cezary's mother was just the right size for it, being small and neat and shiny-faced. She wore her hair in plaits on top of her head.

As usual, the boys sat on the blue bench outside the cottage. Cezary's mother brought them mugs of tea and, looking at Oliver's pale face, a big plate of toast. Cheerio lay hopefully at their feet.

Only when they'd eaten all the toast and Cheerio had been allowed a crust from each of them, did Oliver begin to tell Cezary about the arrival of A.C. Hennessy, and how he knew it was against Pa's rule about strangers, but Ma had been so happy to have a famous author in the house – and after all, she was a guest, wasn't she? A guest someone *invited* couldn't be the same as a stranger, could she? And Lottie . . . well, Lottie seemed to have a bit of a crush on her – and Titch was in love with Amber.

'Amber?' queried Cezary.

'Her horse,' said Oliver. 'Amber is a rather beautiful chestnut horse. It's very hard *not* to love Amber.'

'And you?' asked Cezary.

'Well, Amber's OK,' said Oliver. 'But Ace –

that's what we call her, Ace . . .'

'She is not beautiful?' said Cezary.

'Well, she is in a way,' said Oliver. 'Only I don't think she's real.'

'Real? What d'you mean, "real"? You think you – what you say – hally-lucy-mate?'

'Hallucinate!' said Oliver, laughing. 'No. I just don't think she is who she says she is.'

'Not a famous author. An in-poster!' exclaimed Cezary.

'Imposter,' corrected Oliver. *And that's it*, he was thinking. *That's the word I've been trying to find to describe her. An imposter.*

Then he told Cezary about his doubts. How Ace didn't write anything. How she kept asking questions about Pa. How she'd taken away the covers of her books. How Biggles hisses at her, and Grandpa's ghosts wouldn't appear for her.

'It's not sounding good,' said Cezary. 'I think we have to check her out.'

'But how?' asked Oliver.

Chapter 8

Finding Out

Perhaps because she'd been given the use of Pa's study, or because she spent at least an hour a day reading to Ma, or because everyone treated her as if she really *was* A.C. Hennessy, the famous author, Moll/Ace found herself beginning to write. Lottie grew quite excited when she poked her nose into the study and saw her scribbling away in the fat notebook Ma had laid out for her.

'Is it a children's story?' asked Lottie. 'Are we in it?'

'Is it about a horse?' Titch wanted to know, when he heard that Ace was in Pa's study, writing.

'Well, you are sort of in it,' said Moll/Ace, 'and there is a horse. But it's not really a story.' At which point Lottie and Titch lost interest.

What Moll was writing was a diary. Being an imposter was really quite hard work, particularly if you didn't really want to be one.

The trouble is, she wrote, *I like them all! In fact, I'm not quite sure who I like most, although I think it might be Titch because he loves Amber and because I'm teaching him to ride. (He can do a trot already.) They have all been very kind – even Oliver who I don't think likes me very much but always offers me a second helping of pudding. Biggles definitely doesn't like me, and I think Grandpa is disappointed in me. He wanted to introduce me to his ghost-friends.*

I suppose it's impossible to deceive cats and ghosts. And I wish I didn't have to deceive the Coggins. This morning I found myself wishing they'd adopt me, which is ridiculous because they're going to hate me when they find out I'm not A.C. Hennessy.

Also I love Dizzy Perch. *It's a crazy old house,
but I love being here, up high among the cliffs
as if we're all birds in a nest. Even Amber likes
it here too. Perhaps the beach is like an Arabian
desert to her. Or she likes having children
around. Both of us are happier here than in that
awful caravan and the boring field.*

*I found the key to Pa's chest just dangling
among Ma's zips and strips of buttons. I think
she meant to put it away and forgot. She hasn't
noticed it's missing. This is it, I thought, and I
was almost sad about it – I'm going to find out
where Pa Coggin is, and probably find copies of
his research papers. And then I'll have to tell
Big Mac, and it will all be over. What he plans to
do to his Sworn Enemy I dread to think. Big
Mac's been convinced that all the answers are
in the chest . . . But they're not! Actually it was
quite a relief. The chest seems half empty as if
someone – Pa Coggin, I suppose – has taken
lots out of it. The important things perhaps. All
that was left was a lot of smelly old clothes, a
couple of rugs and a squashed hat. At the*

bottom, under the clothes, were some coils of rope, a first aid kit, a Swiss army knife, and a Gotcha rescue kit. For what? No papers. No notebooks and definitely no maps. And nothing about the location of the Coggins laboratory. There's been mention of a laboratory by both Oliver and Grandpa, but whenever I've asked where it is, they both shut up. Do they know?

Last night Big Mac screamed at me 'Of course they know, girl! You just haven't won their trust yet.' Maybe I haven't, and it will be awful if I do because then I'll betray them. I have to close my eyes and think of Amber or I could never do this. Sometimes I think I could stand it if Big Mac sold Amber. If she went to a good home, that is. What I really fear is that he'll just not buy her any food. He'll starve her until I do exactly as he wants.

I wish there was someone I could talk to. I suppose it kind of helps to write all this down, but a human being would be better. I don't think Big Mac's patience is going to last much longer. He stomped off to bed last night saying

'Just find out where that Sworn Enemy of ours is. Or else . . .'

I wanted to say, 'Well, he's not my Sworn Enemy,' *but I didn't. It was that* 'Or else . . .' *that gave me the shivers.*

There's something else giving me the shivers. Some days I'm not quite sure if I'm Moll or Ace. What if I'm turning into A.C. Hennessy? Could that happen? Maybe it is happening already and that's why I'm writing a diary. Writing! As if I'm Ace.

'We need to go to the library,' said Cezary. 'There's a library in Brochmuir. My Dad took me there when we moved here. We borrowed an English dictionary until we had enough money to buy one.'

'How's the library going to help us?' asked Oliver.

'They may have A.C. Hennessy's books, stupid,' said Cezary, 'and they have big books about famous people. They tell you all about them. There's one called *Who's Who.*'

'Sounds like an owl,' said Oliver. 'And how d'you know about it?'

'Dad wanted to find out about somebody famous and the library lady gave him *Who's Who* to look at. Then he started looking up all sorts of famous people. I thought we'd never get home.'

'Brochmuir's miles away,' said Oliver. 'How did you get there?'

'Well, ten miles,' said Cezary. 'We went on the bus. Have you got any money?'

'No,' said Oliver. 'Not unless I borrow some of the shopping money and Ma is keeping a careful watch on that.'

'Me neither,' said Cezary sadly.

And then both of them said: 'Stan!'

They found Stan inside the cab of Bus Number X254, winding the handle to change the destination printed on the front from STARWATER to LOCH WARDLE.

'Morning, boys!' he called, climbing out. 'Tea break,' he said, flourishing a silver flask and sitting down on the step of the bus.

Stan was a skinny man with a thin thatch of once-blonde hair and bright button eyes. As usual he was wearing a checked shirt with the sleeves rolled up and with a brown leather pouch fixed to his belt.

Oliver knew the bus well. Last year when he'd had to go and find Pa in his Highland laboratory, he'd been on the bus all the way to Loch Wardle, and on the way he'd confided in Stan about how Pa was working on something secret and important, but that he'd forgotten to come home. And Stan had been very sympathetic. He'd shared his cake and lemonade with Oliver. 'Something about the oldest son,' Stan had said. 'Always has to take charge in the end.' And somehow that had given Oliver courage to go on alone up the steep, rough path to Auchterlaldy.

He was remembering this now as he and Cezary hovered round the bus. It was an old, rackety bus, but much loved. Oliver found himself thinking that Stan loved his bus almost in the same way as Ace loved Amber.

'Well, was there something?' asked Stan, eyeing them with his sharp bright eyes. 'It's not that Pa of yours again is it, Olly? Some fathers are such a lot of trouble.'

The boys laughed. 'No,' said Oliver. 'It's just that we need to go to the library in Brochmuir . . .'

'And we haven't any money,' finished Cezary.

'And might this be an educational visit?' enquired Stan.

'Not exactly,' said Oliver. And within minutes, and because there was something so kindly about Stan that you felt he'd look after your most secret secret, he'd told him all about the famous author A.C. Hennessy, and how he thought Ace wasn't her.

Then Cezary chipped in with, 'We think she's an imposter. We need to check her out in the library.'

'She keeps asking questions about Pa,' said Oliver. 'And Biggles hates her.'

'Well, that settles it, doesn't it?' said Stan.

'Hop in. I think we're just doing a little extra journey. The library in Brochmuir did you say?'

'Yes!' they shouted.

It took Stan a few goes at the ignition for the engine to catch and a judder to go through the whole bus as if it was just waking up from a very deep sleep.

'Here we go then,' said Stan. 'This could be an imposter-busting mission.'

Chapter 9

Whoever You Are

Brochmuir wasn't a town and it wasn't a village. It was something in between. It had one of everything. One High Street (with a row of shops), one school (divided into primary and secondary), one church, one doctor's surgery, one pub, and one library.

Stan had dropped them off by the church. 'I've got passengers to collect,' he explained. 'I can't let them down. I'll come back for you in two hours. Here's a pound each – get yourselves something to eat. Good luck!' And with a toot of his horn – the horn of Bus Number X254 sounded as if it had a sore throat – he was off.

To Oliver, who really only knew *Dizzy Perch*

and Starwater, Brochmuir seemed big and noisy.

'So many people!' he said. 'Do they all live cramped up together? And all these shops! How do we find the library?'

Cezary laughed. 'You country boy,' he said. 'I come from big city. Gdansk is – is . . .' Cezary spread his arms as wide as they could go. 'Five, ten, twenty times bigger than Brochmuir. Big port. Big ships. Big buildings. Big.'

'Oh,' said Oliver, feeling rather small. 'And you like it?'

'It's proper home,' said Cezary. 'Big city exciting.' And shoving his hands in his pockets, his walk took on a little swagger. 'Now we find the library.'

Home, thought Oliver, *Does everyone have a proper home? If it's the place where you really, really belong then Pa's home is in his Highland laboratory, and Ma's home seems to be in a book.* And with almost a homesick ache – because after all, he was only about ten miles away – he suddenly felt a longing for *Dizzy*

Perch, where you woke every morning listening to the sea and the gulls and the wind rattling the shutters, and Grandpa playing his fiddle.

'I'm not a country boy,' he panted, hurrying after Cezary. 'I'm a sea boy.'

And then he wondered if Cezary felt homesick a lot of the time because he was far, far, far away from Poland and Gdansk.

'We both sea boys,' said Cezary. 'But today we library boys. Here it is.'

Brochmuir Library was a small, one-storey sandstone building with a date – *1899* – carved above its entrance. The door had a shiny brass handle and letterbox, both looking as if they'd just been polished. Oliver wiped his hands down his trousers. Cezary combed his hair with his fingers, and pulled his T-shirt straight.

'After you,' said Oliver.

But beyond the main door there was another revolving door and they both went round and round five times until they saw a young woman, her hands on her hips, watching them and laughing.

'Are you planning to come in?' she asked.

She held the door still until they tumbled out, blushing and a little dizzy.

'I'm Emily Pye,' she said. 'The librarian. Can I help you?'

Emily Pye was all of twenty years old. She wore a jaunty kilt that swung from her hips when she walked, as if she might begin to dance at any minute. To accompany the jaunty kilt was a jaunty ponytail tied up with a red ribbon. And behind her little round brown spectacles were round brown eyes, still laughing at them.

'Well . . .' said Oliver. He thought she was the prettiest person he'd ever seen.

'Well . . .' said Cezary, who thought exactly the same thing at exactly the same moment.

'I imagine you want a book,' said Emily Pye. 'Do you have library cards?'

'No,' said Oliver. 'How do we get one?'

'I can do that for you,' said Emily Pye, taking them over to the counter.

'You can?' said Cezary. 'One each perhaps.'

'Well, yes, if that's what you'd like,' said

114

Emily Pye, and she took out two forms and began filling them in with their names and addresses.

'*Dizzy Perch*,' she said. 'That's a strange address. Now, we have a children's section and an adult section. And we have fiction and non-fiction. Was there a particular book you wanted?'

'Do you have anything by A.C. Hennessy?' asked Oliver.

'Oh my! A.C. Hennessy! I adore her books,' said Emily Pye. 'A bit old for you, I would have thought. Perhaps for your mother? Do you have one or two?'

'Books or mothers?' asked Oliver. He wondered about saying something about the red ribbon in her hair and how cheery it was to look at. Would that be polite? Would it please her? He decided not to risk it.

'Mothers,' said Emily Pye. 'Because you don't look alike.'

'Two,' said Cezary. 'We have two mothers. One each.'

'It's mine who likes A.C. Hennessy,' said Oliver. 'In fact just at the moment we have Ace . . .'

But Cezary nudged him in the ribs. 'Better not,' he whispered. 'Do our research first.'

'Well,' said Emily Pye, 'we only have three books by A.C. Hennessy, but I can show you those if you like.'

'Please,' said Oliver. He felt himself growing very hot. Was he about to make a complete fool of himself? Emily Pye adored A.C. Hennessy. Anyone Emily Pye adored must be OK.

Emily led them over to the adult fiction shelves, ran her finger along the middle shelf that ran from E to J, pulled out three books and laid them on the table.

'There,' she said. 'Have a look at those while I go and make your library cards.'

Two of the books were ones that Oliver had seen at home – *Adventure in the Outback* and *Jenny Penny Finds a Way*. The third was *What the Heart Knows*. All three books still wore their dust jackets and the inside flap

of all three dust jackets was exactly the same.
There were only a few lines of writing.

A.C. Hennessy, Oliver and Cezary read,
has written ninety-four novels.
('Ninety-four!' breathed Oliver, horrified.)
*She has won the Critchley Prize and
the Long Knottery Prize, and is three
times winner of the Romantic Novelists
Heartache prize.*

On the back of the dust jackets were quotations
from people who had read the book:

'*A page turner from beginning to end.*'
'*Hennessy in her usual top form.*'
'*No one can make you laugh and cry like
Hennessy does.*'

Both boys shut the books and looked at each
other. Oliver felt more like crying than laughing.
'It doesn't tell us anything,' he said. Not
even what A and C stands for. It's no help.'

117

'What's no help?' asked Emily Pye, coming over to the table with their new library cards.

'We wanted to find out more about A.C. Hennessy,' said Cezary. 'Do you have a book called *Who's Who?*'

'We do indeed,' said Emily Pye. 'I suppose you're doing all this for your mothers?'

'Sort of,' said Oliver.

'I can show you *Who's Who*,' said Emily, 'but I doubt if it will be much help. I happen to know that A.C. Hennessy is something of a recluse.'

'A recluse?' asked Oliver.

'Someone who lives alone and doesn't really like mixing with people,' said Emily. She led them over to the reference section, and pulled out *Who's Who*. 'See for yourselves,' she said.

And they did. The reference for A.C. Hennessy took all of six lines, and said even less than the dust jackets.

A.C. Hennessy has written ninety-four books, most of them romantic novels. Regarded mostly as a writer passionate about privacy, she has never been interviewed and has refused all requests to visit festivals or colleges. Her publishers are Hubert & Busters, 167 Nitchin Street, London WC2 4AE.

Oliver closed the book. 'So that's that!' he said.

'Don't you see?' shouted Cezary jumping up, and making Emily Pye point to the sign that said *Silence*. 'That's proof! A.C. Hennessy never goes anywhere. So how can she be at *Dizzy Perch*?'

'That's proof to us,' said Oliver. 'But it isn't proof to Ma. Ma believes Ace is A.C. Hennessy. Lottie believes it. Titch believes it. Grandpa believes it.' Oliver felt close to tears.

'We can't just give up,' said Cezary. 'Perhaps we can borrow *Who's Who* on our library cards?'

'I'm afraid not,' said Emily Pye. 'It's a reference book. We have to keep it here for anyone to consult. You could write out what it says though.' She went back to her counter and produced paper and pens and, to help them along, two chocolate biscuits and a glass each of lemonade.

They took it in turns to do the writing. Oliver was quicker than Cezary because although Cezary's English was good, he still found writing it quite difficult. They were glad of the chocolate biscuits – and of the clock above Emily's counter.

'Two hours is nearly up,' said Cezary. 'We'd better go if we don't want to miss Stan.'

Oliver just had time to finish writing out the publisher's address, to thank Emily Pye for her help and to pocket their new library cards before they had to dash.

'Come again,' Emily Pye called after them as they spun, for the last time, round the revolving door.

They'd managed to stop at a chip shop and get three pokes of chips with the money Stan had given them, when they heard the familiar sound of Bus Number X254 coming round the corner and hooting as it came. They got to the church just as the bus drew in, stopped and shook and rattled for a full minute before the engine fell silent.

'Success?' asked Stan, jumping out. 'Chips for me? Grand! Have we busted the imposter?'

'We have and we haven't,' said Oliver.

Stan sat them in the front of the bus, and in between dipping their fingers into the pokes of chips, they told him all about A.C. Hennessy's ninety-four books, and what they'd read about her in *Who's Who*, and how they'd copied it all out, and wasn't Emily Pye pretty? And, well, A.C. Hennessy was a recluse and never visited anyone, so that was proof wasn't it?

'Only, I don't think they'll believe me,' said Oliver. 'Ma and Lottie and Titch and Grandpa. Even when they read what I've written, I don't think they'll believe me. You see I think they're all – well – I think they're all in love with her!'

'Whoever you've got up there in *Dizzy Perch* is a terrible cheat,' said Stan, looking very stern. He started up the engine and let it run a little until its splutters were soothed and its engine ran smooth. 'There's only one thing more you can do,' said Stan.

'What?' asked Oliver and Cezary together.

'You've got the publisher's address,' said Stan. 'Write to A.C. Hennessy at the publishers. Tell her what's happened. I bet three bags of chips she won't be at all happy about someone pretending to be her. I bet you three bags of chips and a bottle of lemonade she'll do something about it.'

'You think so?' asked Oliver.

'I'm sure so,' said Stan and he gave two extra-loud toots on the horn.

Several pedestrians looked up in alarm.

Chapter 10

Big Mac's Awful Plan

Big Mac had terrible indigestion. It was Moll's fault. She was very late home and he'd had to make his own supper. There was a small battery-operated fridge, a food cupboard, and a bread bin in the caravan. Big Mac investigated all three. Cooking was beyond him. He ate a tin of baked beans (cold), a rather old doughnut, a whole packet of chocolate biscuits, a bottle of Irn Bru, two scones, three bananas and a large slab of cheese.

It was a balmy night. Big Mac saw bats flitting past him in the dusk. In the far distance he could hear voices coming up from the harbour at Starwater and the low moan of a boat coming in for the night. Big Mac sat on the step of the caravan in his purple and pink pyjamas and matching nightcap, burping, and feeling both cross and sorry for himself.

Most nights, Big Mac couldn't get to sleep for thoughts of his Sworn Enemy. Sometimes he pictured him shaking hands with the Queen. Sometimes he pictured him surrounded by newspaper men holding out microphones to catch his every word. Such thoughts, plus his indigestion and the lateness of Moll, did nothing to improve his temper. Where was Moll? And when was she going to come back from *Dizzy Perch* with some useful information?

Big Mac's burps woke up a visiting owl. The owl gave a hoot of protest.

Moll had stayed late at *Dizzy Perch* because it had been a music night, and Titch had said *please please PLEASE* would she come along. Telling herself that Big Mac could just wait for his supper, Ace/Moll said she'd be delighted.

And it had been a lovely evening. Squashed

124

up on one of the sofas in the sitting room between Titch and Lottie, she'd felt as if she'd become one of the family, had turned into a Coggin.

Everyone did a turn. Grandpa played his fiddle and Lottie danced a highland sword dance between two walking sticks crossed over. She was very neat and nimble. Titch was persuaded to do his tap dance, Oliver recited a poem called 'Sea Fever', and Ma half read and half sang 'A Red Red Rose'.

'She's not really singing it to us,' Grandpa whispered to Ace/Moll. 'She's singing it to him, you know.'

'Pa,' said Ace/Moll, as Ma's singing brought the tears to her eyes.

> *'Till a' the seas gang dry, my dear,*
> *And the rocks melt wi' the sun;*
> *I will love thee still, my dear,*
> *While the sands o' life shall run.'*

sang Ma. *Oh dear*, thought Ace/Moll. *Big Mac's*

Sworn Enemy is Ma's true love. This is awful.

'Your turn,' said Grandpa. 'Can you sing us a song?'

Straight away a song popped into Ace/Moll's head. *Maybe this will help them guess*, she thought. *Please, please, please will someone find me out!*

> 'Early one morning,' sang Ace/Moll,
> 'Just as the sun was rising,
> I heard a maid a-singing
> In the valley below.
> "Oh don't deceive me,
> Oh never leave me,
> How could you use
> a poor maiden so?"'

'What a very interesting song to choose,' said Oliver. 'A song about deceiving people.'

'She sang it very nicely,' Grandpa said, and everyone clapped.

Down in her cave-stable, Amber whinnied impatiently.

Whatever I do, I can't get it right, thought Ace/Moll. *If they find me out, Big Mac will be furious and punish Amber. If they don't find me out, I'll be betraying them all.*

'I'd better go,' she said. 'I'll see you all in the morning.'

Everyone – everyone except Oliver – hugged her.

It was almost midnight when she left. The hugs kept her warm as Amber galloped along the beach. It was a wonderful ride under the moon. She passed round the back of Starwater, and realised how the village got its name, for although the tide was rolled far back, the stars looked as if they'd fallen in the water and it would be the easiest thing in the world to fish one out.

She was hoping Big Mac would be asleep. But he wasn't. Even as she neared the caravan, she could see the light from the oil lamp in the caravan window. Moll's heart sank.

Big Mac seemed to explode out of the caravan like a large purple and pink balloon. Amber was so startled that she almost rose up on her back legs, and Moll had to quickly pat her flanks to calm her down.

'I suppose you know I've had to make my own supper,' roared Big Mac. 'Me with my delicate constitution. Oh what d'you care? What d'you care?' Big Mac mopped his eyes with his night cap.

'I hope you're late because you've got news for me,' he said, 'because I'm tired of waiting. Very tired, d'you understand? The longer this goes on, the more likely it is that he-who-shall-be-nameless will end up earning a fortune from his research, and winning a Nobel Prize. It's unbearable!'

'I'm very sorry . . .' Moll began.

'Sorry!' shouted Big Mac. 'That's all I hear from you. Sorry. Well, I'll tell you what you've got to do. Bring one of those little Coggins here, the littlest will do – that will get us a result.'

Moll felt cold all over, as if someone had tipped a bucket of ice over her.

'I won't do it,' she said.

'Shame about that nag of yours,' said Big Mac. 'Is that her last bag of oats?'

The next day, back in Starwater, Oliver and Cezary sat on the floor in Cezary's tiny bedroom and began writing a letter to A.C. Hennessy.

'D'you think she's Miss or Mrs?' asked Oliver.

'We could just say *Dear Madam*,' said Cezary. 'You need to put your address first.'

Dizzy Perch,
   Near Starwater,
   Scotland

wrote Oliver in his best handwriting. Then,

Dear Madam,
   We think we have an imposter living in our house. She says her name is A.C. Hennessy, but we think it isn't really you. We looked you up - that is, my friend Cezary and I - in a book called Who's Who in the library. It didn't tell us very much, but

Emily Pye who you may know because she is the librarian and looks after all the books and likes yours very much, says that you are a recluse, which I think means you never come out. That sounds a bit lonely to me, but maybe you don't mind.

'I'm not sure you should put that in,' said Cezary.

'I can't just cross it out and I can't start again,' said Oliver. 'They'll be expecting me at home.'

Anyway, he continued, my mother is a great fan of yours. In fact, she might be your greatest fan because although she's only got eight of your books, and I know you've written ninety-four, which is amazing, she reads them over and over and over. She keeps them in a special shopping basket by her bed.

The lady who I think is pretending to be you has a horse called Amber. So unless you have a horse called Amber, she can't be you, can she? I think she is trying to find out where my father is. My father is a very important scientist called Amos Coggin and he is away in his secret laboratory in the Highlands doing important research. Lots of people want to steal his work, which is why we all live in Dizzy Perch which is high up in the cliffs above the sea, but Pa (Amos Coggin) thinks we'll all be safe there.

The trouble is that the rest of my family – that is, Ma, Titch (my little brother), Lottie (my little sister), and Grandpa all love the lady pretending to be you. It is up to me to tell them the truth before she finds out where my pa is living. If someone finds him, I don't know what they'll do. I'm afraid they might hurt him.

Please write to me and tell me that you are the real A.C. Hennessy and that you don't have a horse called Amber. A postcard will do. I don't want to interrupt your writing or stop you being a recluse.

Yours sincerely,
Oliver Coggin

Cezary's mother gave them an envelope, and Cezary addressed it, very carefully, to *A.C. Hennessy, Care of Hubert & Busters, 167 Nitchin Street, London WC2 4AE*. They just had enough from the money Stan had given them to take the letter down to the Post Office Stores and buy a first class stamp.

Mrs Tansley put on her postmistress hat when they came in. She opened a big book of stamps and took one out for them.

'Well,' she said, 'if it isn't that famous author again! A.C. Hennessy. But now you've got an address – or sort of. That looks like the publishers.'

'It is,' said Oliver.

Mrs Tansley stuck the stamp on and dropped the letter in the box behind her counter.

'I gave the last letter to that second cousin of yours,' she said.

'Second cousin?' said Oliver.

'Yes, you know the lady with the golden hair – bit like a horse's mane. She was off to see you all at *Dizzy Perch*. She did arrive, didn't she?'

Mrs Tansley leaned over the counter looking quite worried.

'I wouldn't like to think she got lost going up the cliffs or something.'

Oliver and Cezary looked at each other.

'Oh yes, she did arrive,' said Oliver.

'That's all right then,' said Mrs Tansley. 'I wouldn't want to think anything had happened to her.'

Chapter 11

Hubert & Busters

It was Hattie who opened the post at Hubert & Busters. Hattie was new. She was hoping to write a novel herself and at home had a drawer full of unfinished stories. In the meantime, she felt very lucky to be working for the publisher Hubert & Busters, where she could spend a good part of every day reading other people's stories and trying to work out which was a good one and which was a bad one.

Apart from opening the post, it was also Hattie's job to return a story when Mr Ernest Gadly read a page and either snorted loudly or shouted 'RUBBISH!' Then he'd toss the manuscript to Hattie (Hattie had learnt to call stories *manuscripts*, which made them sound as if they hadn't been written by a person but by an invisible hand) saying, 'Usual rejection slip, Hats.'

The rejection slips were nasty little things, about the size of a postcard. The ones from Hubert & Busters said:

> *Thank you for submitting your story*
> *to Hubert & Busters. The editor regrets*
> *he is unable to publish it.*

That was all. Not even a *Dear So-and-So*. Or *We can't publish your story because we've got too many*. Or *What good characters! I really like Megan*, or *Bill*, or *the Italian Count who rescues them both*.

As often as she could, Hattie added a little note of her own. '*I liked your story even if Mr Gadly didn't. He is awfully difficult to please, so don't be too hurt,*' she wrote.

There was always a lot of post in the morning. Hattie thought there must be hundreds of people writing stories and sending them to Hubert & Busters. Hattie put the new fat manuscripts in one pile and the letters in another.

Over his coffee, Mr Gadly sat at his big desk (that somehow stayed messy even though Hattie tried to tidy it every night) looking through the new manuscripts and talking to them as if their senders were sitting beside him.

'Well, Andrew St Clare Newman, I do believe! And about time too! What did it say in your contract? January, wasn't it?'

'Ah! Here's Tabitha Morris. Now if this is a new story it's sure to be a bestseller.'

Mostly what he said was 'Slush pile, Hats!' which was where all the stories by unknown writers went, and which, once every three or six months Mr Gadly, heaving a huge sigh, took off home to read, sometimes bringing one back to say 'This is a good 'un!'

It was also Hattie's job to open the ordinary, slim letters, to take them out of their envelopes, smooth them nicely, and lay them out for Mr

Gadly to read. Sometimes there were letters from readers who really liked one or other of Hubert & Busters' books. Sometimes there was a letter about a prize, or a newspaper article about a Hubert & Buster author.

Mr Gadly had his nose in the new story by Tabitha Morris when Hattie came upon Oliver's letter to A.C. Hennessy. Hattie knew about A.C. Hennessy. She could hardly not know. On her very first day, she'd been told that Hennessy was Hubert & Buster's top selling novelist, that she'd written ninety-four novels – one, sometimes two a year – and they very much hoped she'd carry on. There were posters showing the covers of her books all over the walls. Hattie had tried to read one or two but had felt terribly bored. She thought it must be her own fault and she should try harder.

'Here's a letter for A.C. Hennessy,' she called over to Mr Gadly. It was a big office, Hattie's desk was in the far corner, so far in the corner she sometimes thought Mr Gadly forgot she was there.

Mr Gadly looked up, tipping his specs up to the top of his head, all the better to see her there. 'Oh bin it!' he said. 'Hennessy never reads letters unless there's one from us with a cheque inside. And she never sees anyone either. Once upon a very long time ago she came into the office. Maybe it was when she was on novel number five. She hasn't been seen since. She's a recluse. Does nothing but write and write and write.'

'How awful!' said Hattie.

'Not for us it isn't,' said Mr Gadly. 'A.C. Hennessy's novels pay my wages, and yours, my girl.'

'It does seem like quite an important letter,' said Hattie. 'The writer says he's got an imposter living with him. Someone pretending to be A.C. Hennessy.'

'There's always someone pretending to be Hennessy,' said Mr Gadly impatiently. 'Like there's always someone pretending to be Elvis.'

'It's from a boy called Oliver. Says his father's an important scientist called Amos Coggin. He thinks this imposter might put him in danger.'

'Amos Coggin? I think I've heard of him. Batty. Probably this is his batty son. Batty, Hattie? Bats! Hats!' said Mr Gadly roaring with laughter. 'Just be a good girl and put it in the bin, will you?'

Hattie didn't laugh. She put the letter at the bottom of the pile and when Mr Gadly went off for lunch, she slipped it into her bag. Somehow the letter seemed to be telling a story which Hattie couldn't get out of her head. *That poor boy*, she thought, *worrying about his Pa*. She could picture the whole family living in this strange house above the cliffs called *Dizzy Perch*. And then this imposter turning up with a horse! A horse called Amber. And it wasn't as if Oliver Coggin was asking much. He just wanted a postcard from the *real* A.C. Hennessy. Hattie thought of writing one herself, but then it wouldn't quite do would it?

Mr Gadly had a long lunch hour. He went to his club or he went to a posh restaurant or sometimes he just went to the corner caff for a poached egg on toast. Wherever he went, he took a long time over it, usually because he had his favourite comic with him. Hattie never said anything about the comic. She'd been about to one day, about to say something like, 'Isn't that for children?', but Mr Gadly had given her such a fierce look, she turned the words into a yawn.

She knew he'd be away long enough for her to look in the filing cabinet. If Mr Gadly sent Hennessy cheques, he must know where to send them. The papers in the filing cabinet had once been in alphabetical order but either someone who didn't know the alphabet or someone who didn't care about order, had left them all mixed up. Hattie resolved that one day when she wasn't too busy, she would sort them out. Right now she had to thumb her way through umpteen loose folders until at last she came upon a very old one labelled *A.C. Hennessy*.

There wasn't a lot inside it. A few flimsy letters and all of them saying the same thing – *Dear Miss Hennessy, I enclose a cheque in payment for* Jenny Penny Finds a Way, (*or* The Star-Crossed Lovers, *or* Beginning to Know Love) *Best wishes, Earnest Gadly*. Hattie wondered if there were ninety-four such letters, one for each of Hennessy's books, but she couldn't be bothered to count them. One thing was clear, A.C. Hennessy had always lived at the same house – Garden Cottage, Parvel, Kent.

Hattie scribbled the address on a rejection slip and put it in her bag alongside Oliver's letter. Hattie was a girl with a strong sense of justice. Oliver deserved a reply, she thought. And who was to say that A.C. Hennessy always wanted to be a recluse? You could often be wrong about people, Hattie thought. Hennessy might – just might – welcome a visitor.

Moll had a sleepless night. Her bed in the hayloft was an old camp bed left over from long-ago holidays. Its mattress was thin and lumpy. Except for one small shutter, the hayloft was dark and warm. Moll kept the one shutter open for both air and light. The moon seemed intent on looking in on her as if to enquire what was up.

She could hear Amber down below in her stable. Perhaps the horse, like the moon, sensed something was wrong.

Moll tossed and turned. When she tossed one way, she pictured Amber getting thinner and thinner until you saw all her bones.

When she tossed the other way, she saw Titch. Titch looking at her as if she'd betrayed him. Titch, kept up here in the hayloft crying for Ma or Oliver or Grandpa, or all of them. And Big Mac being scary.

After he'd given her his ultimatum to kidnap 'the littlest Coggin' or see Amber starve, Big Mac rushed back into the caravan and in a fury that seemed to tie knots in his hair, had written the ransom note. He'd done it in big angry red capital letters and waved it in her face. The ransom note read:

TO ALL AT *DIZZY PERCH*
IF YOU WANT YOUR BOY BACK

UNHARMED
REVEAL ADDRESS OF
COGGIN (PROF.)

Thinking of Titch crying made Moll cry. The tears wetting her skimpy pillow made her realise how fond she'd become of him. He'd won her heart by loving Amber. Every morning it had been Titch waiting for her, ready to send down the funicular and then to wait, impatiently, while she read to Ma and talked to Grandpa, until she was ready to give him a riding lesson. Amber too had grown fond of Titch, nuzzling his neck when he brought her a carrot or half an apple, and standing very still when Titch brushed the snowy fringes on her legs.

Of course, Moll told herself, wiping her eyes, it wasn't fair to have a favourite, and she liked them all, really she did, but there was just something special about Titch. Then she remembered him tap dancing and cried some more.

Round about three a.m., when the moon was

sliding down the sky, half-lidded like an eye, Moll began wondering if . . . if she *must* kidnap someone (and it looked as if she must), then might it be one of the others?

Moll counted them on her fingers. Lottie? Lottie had a scream that could hurt your eardrums. Oliver? No. Oliver suspected her. Also, he was strong. She'd never manage Oliver. Grandpa? Now who on earth would kidnap a Grandpa and what would Big Mac make of it if she did? Ma? Well, that was just silly!

And at last, Moll fell asleep.

Someone else was having a sleepless night. Hattie. Half a dozen times Hattie sat up in bed and reread Oliver's letter. Really, she thought, it was better than half the stories she read in the office of Hubert & Busters! And she pictured this family, high up in the cliffs in a house called *Dizzy Perch*, living with a wicked witch – no, no, a wicked *imposter* – while somewhere in the Highlands (*How romantic*, Hattie thought) was a famous scientist, and there was this nice boy called Oliver trying to save him! Well, someone, somewhere, had to do something about it!

Very early the next morning – it was a Saturday – Hattie put on her leathers, slipped Oliver's letter and A.C. Hennessy's address in her pocket, got on the back of her Harley Davidson, and roared off.

Chapter 12

The Real A.C. Hennessy

Perhaps it was because she was short of sleep, but Moll had woken up angry. Angry, as usual, with Big Mac, but suddenly very angry with Ma. After all, wasn't it Ma's fault that all this had happened? Ma who'd gone and married Amos Coggin, instead of Big Mac? Ma who'd got this obsession with A.C. Hennessy? Ma who spent all her time reading books, instead of talking to her children? 'Dear Heart' Ma, who wasn't a dear heart at all! Ma who'd made Moll pretend she was someone she wasn't, and caused her so much confusion that from time to time she wasn't sure if she was Moll or Ace.

Enough! thought Moll, galloping Amber

along the beach to *Dizzy Perch* the next morning. Enough! No way was she going to kidnap Titch or Lottie or Oliver or Grandpa. It had to be Ma. All she had to do was get Ma on Amber's back.

Alicia Charlotte Hennessy had not always been a recluse. It had happened slowly or as she put it, 'it had come upon her'. After her true love, Mr Charles Heathcliffe Hennessy, had died – some thirty years ago, when he was still a young man – Alicia, having to earn her living, had begun scribbling stories. Of course she had needed a lot of peace and quiet in order to do so. *Get on with it, girl*, she told herself every morning, after she'd had a little cry for Charles Heathcliffe Hennessy. The better to get on with it, and so that there wouldn't be too many interruptions, she'd moved from a little two-up-two-down in town, to Garden Cottage.

Garden Cottage was more garden than cottage and, as the postman muttered to himself, reluctantly trudging down the muddy lane, it was *the back of beyond*. Not that he had much trudging to do these days, because somehow the word had spread – perhaps from Mr Gadly or perhaps because Alicia forgot to answer any letters or perhaps because she didn't have a telephone – that A.C. Hennessy was a recluse.

It was a mistake. Alicia had never intended becoming a recluse. It had happened like the ivy round the walls of Garden Cottage. Silence, aloneness had spread year after year, had spread round her until her voice was almost a whisper and her feet hardly made a sound.

It's possible that Mr Gadly encouraged it. They had met, once, when Alicia's fifth book had sold a million copies. 'Get on with it, girl!' Mr Gadly had said, echoing Alicia's advice to herself. Alicia blinked once or twice, went away and did just that, so that now she was on her ninety-fifth novel.

'All this time waiting for rescue,' Alicia said out loud. Alicia was seventy-five. Being a recluse-by-mistake had made her just a little loopy. She talked – or whispered – to herself a lot and her memory wasn't too good. She woke up every morning wondering if rescue would come but she could no longer remember what she wanted rescue *from*. Sometimes she thought it was from growing her own vegetables which took an awful lot of effort now that her back wasn't so good and she couldn't dig as well as before. Sometimes she thought it was from silence – but then it wasn't always silent in Garden Cottage. There were plenty of birds. A regular robin. A nesting blackbird. Lots of sparrows. Sometimes, very late at night, it was so silent that she thought she could hear the cottage breathing.

Just now and again, she thought what she wanted rescuing from was writing another book, but she had no idea how that might happen. Alicia wrote books like some people smoke or drink. She was addicted. Only now and then did she dream of all the things she might do instead. Sailing. Mountaineering. Playing the piano in a jazz band.

That Saturday morning, Alicia put novel ninety-five (*Too Late for Love*) in an envelope and addressed it to *E. Gadly Esq., Hubert & Busters*. At the end of the lane where the milkman left a bottle twice a week there was a postbox in the wall. She put the envelope on the table by the back door, to be posted later. Then she made herself a large mug of tea, added four teaspoons of sugar, and took it up to the attic which was her workroom. There was always an uncomfortable lull of a week or two between the end of one book and the beginning of another.

The attic contained all ninety-four of her novels with translations in Chinese, Japanese, French, German, Italian, Hebrew, Urdu, Greek, and Arabic. The books took up all four walls of the attic and made the room rather dark and gloomy. A small window looked out towards the hills of Pawmoor which that morning were just beginning to show a spread of daffodils.

'*I look to the hills from whence cometh my help*,' quoted Alicia Charlotte Hennessy. 'Only it doesn't,' she added sadly. Then she sat down in her swivel chair and swivelled a few times, thinking it might improve her mood.

She was just feeling ever so slightly dizzy when she heard a great roaring noise. It seemed to be coming closer and closer.

'Good heavens!' cried Alicia. 'The roaring of wings! The sound of a hundred angels!' (Even at seventy-five, her imagination was still quite strong). Alarmed, and feeling that a hundred angels was not what she might want by way of rescue, she put her hands over her ears, hid under her desk and waited for the roaring to stop.

When it did, she heard something she hadn't heard for a long time. Footsteps. And not the usual *clump-clump* of the postman. Someone struggling through the bramble bushes to get to the front door. Alicia held her breath. Then came a loud knock. And another! And another!

This is it! thought Alicia joyfully, *Rescue has come*. And as fast as her old legs would carry her, she ran down the stairs. It had been so long since she'd opened the front door (the back one being easy) that it had become very stiff. She had to give it such a good tug she almost fell over backwards, and the person outside had to grab hold of her before she fell on her bottom.

'Oh, a dark angel!' cried Alicia and would have shut the door on her, only Hattie removed her helmet and, showing a tumble of curls, said, 'I'm Hattie. From Hubert & Busters.'

Alicia was a little disappointed. 'I suppose you've come from that Mr Gadfly,' she said. 'And he's wanting another novel. Well, I've got it here for him. He doesn't usually send someone.'

'It's Mr Gadly,' said Hattie. 'And I haven't and he didn't – send me,' she added.

'You'd better come in,' said Alicia. 'I was hoping you'd come to rescue me.'

'Well, in a manner of speaking, I have,' said Hattie. 'At least, there's someone I was hoping *you* might rescue.'

'Me? Rescue someone else?' Alicia was

astonished. 'No one ever quite wants me,' she said. 'They just want another book. Are you sure Mr Gadfly didn't send you?'

'Positive,' said Hattie. 'Mr Gadly doesn't know I'm here.'

Alicia sat down at her kitchen table. The presence of someone else in the house was quite a shock.

'Who is it you want me to rescue?' she asked. She felt her voice getting just a little stronger.

'A boy,' said Hattie. 'A boy called Oliver.'

What Moll hadn't expected was that the others – Oliver, Lottie, Titch, Grandpa – would all help. Of course they weren't to know what was in her head.

'I really need to teach you to ride,' she told Ma. 'It's for a story,' she said. (This wasn't altogether a lie. Apart from her diary, Moll had begun a story set in *Dizzy Perch. This is what comes of pretending to be A.C. Hennessy*, she told herself.)

'I need a heroine,' she said. (This was a lie.)

'Someone who gallops into the sunset.' (This wasn't.)

The Coggins were eating lunch.

'What a splendid idea,' said Grandpa. 'Can I be in the story too?'

'And me,' said Titch.

'And me,' said Lottie.

'No,' said Moll/Ace. 'Maybe you can be in a different story.' (Really, was there no end to this story business?)

Oliver said nothing. *What was Ace up to now?* he wondered. Well, persuading Ma to get some fresh air couldn't be that bad. And after lunch he was going to hurry down to the Post Office in Starwater, to see if there was a reply to his letter. Cezary would be expecting him.

'I need a heroine with a sense of adventure,' Moll said.

'Dear Thing,' said Ma, half flattered, half cross, 'you know I never go out if I can help it. Surely you can imagine a heroine?'

'It won't be the same,' pleaded Moll. 'And I really want it to be you. You'd look so fine on

Amber's back. If you could wear that blue cloak of yours? And maybe the sombrero with a feather in it – the one hanging on the bedknob?'

'Is it to be a Western?' asked Ma, warming to the idea.

'Possibly,' said Moll.

'Oh do it do it do it!' cried Titch.

'I'll fetch your cloak,' said Lottie.

'It could do you the world of good,' said Grandpa. 'Getting out in the sunshine. Getting some exercise.'

'Dear Things,' said Ma. 'If it would please you all. And for the sake of literature. I'll do it!'

'Hurray!' they all shouted, even Oliver, and in no time at all, Ma was dressed in her blue cloak with her sombrero on her head and the boots she hadn't worn for at least five years, and was sailing down in the funicular with Titch on her lap and Moll/Ace on the chair beside her.

Oliver, Grandpa and Lottie were next on the funicular with Lottie on Grandpa's lap.

It was a beautiful May afternoon. All the promise of spring in the air and the tide rolled back, shiny as a brand new roll of tinfoil. Up on the cliffs a congregation of snowy-white gannets arranged themselves like an audience.

Amber was led out from her cave-stable by Titch, and given half an apple.

'She's quite big,' Ma said nervously.

'Fourteen hands,' said Titch promptly. 'That's how you measure a horse.'

'You'll need a leg up,' said Grandpa.

'We'll help,' said Titch and Lottie.

'I shall get on first,' said Moll, 'then you help Ma on behind me.'

Everyone was so eager to help that Ma didn't have time to protest. Grandpa made a stirrup from his hands. Oliver, Titch and Lottie all heaved Ma from behind until – with a *FERLUMPH* and an 'Oh my goodness' – she was sitting behind Moll, one arm round Moll's waist, one arm holding on to her hat.

'Dear Thing, we don't have to go anywhere, do we?' she wailed.

But she was too late. Moll didn't waste any time. Gently she pressed her foot into Amber's side as the signal to go. Instantly Amber was alert. Twice more Moll touched the horse's side. It was the signal for gallop.

And they were off.

'Yahiiiiii!' screeched Ma. And that was the last they heard of her. The sand flew up from Amber's hooves. Ma's sombrero flew off. Its feather took to the cliffs as if seeking whatever bird it had once belonged to.

Dumbstruck, Grandpa, Oliver, Titch, and Lottie stood staring after them. They could see Ma was no longer upright on Amber's back, but somehow lying sideways, her bottom in the air, her legs waving.

'She'll be back soon,' said Titch, his voice quivering a little.

'Now she's lost her cloak,' said Lottie, and she buried her face in Grandpa's chest.

'I'm going to wait here until she comes back,' said Titch.

But though he sat on the beach until it was way past supper time and almost ready for the sun to set, there was no sign of Ma.

Oliver persuaded him to come back up to *Dizzy Perch*. He had abandoned his plan of going to the Post Office Stores. Everyone was in need of comfort. And food.

Over supper, he tried to tell them that he suspected Ace was an imposter and had only come to *Dizzy Perch* to find out where Pa had gone.

'I think she's deceived us all,' said Oliver. How much dare he tell them? They might all hate him for telling them the truth.

'No,' said Titch loyally, 'I don't believe it. I love her and Amber. And I think she loves me.'

'I'm sorry,' said Oliver. 'I should never have let her stay in the beginning. We all know what Pa told us.'

'No strangers,' said Lottie mournfully. 'But she's become a friend.' Lottie didn't plan on telling anyone about her daydream that Moll was her real mother-princess. Now it turned out Ace wasn't real at all. It was the most awful thing that had ever happened.

'The thing is,' said Grandpa, 'where has she taken Ma?'

At which point Titch's tears made his chips all soggy.

Chapter 13

Hattie and Hennessy

'Well, that's a lovely story,' said Alicia when Hattie had finished telling her all about Oliver and the Coggin family; how they lived in a house high in the cliffs called *Dizzy Perch*, and their father was a famous scientist who might be in danger and there was this woman with a horse called Amber who was really an imposter.

'Very good,' said Alicia, clapping her hands. 'A splendid story. You should write it down. Or maybe I could borrow it for my ninety-sixth . . . ?'

'This isn't a story!' cried Hattie. 'This is real life. Look!'

'Real life,' whispered Alicia in a tone of awe.

'I'm not very used to that.'

'Look!' said Hattie. And she laid Oliver's letter on the table in front of Alicia.

'Oh dear, oh dear!' said Alicia, when she'd read it. 'This is dreadful. Someone pretending to be me! That poor boy and his poor, poor mother who is obviously my fan – deceived. All of them deceived! Seduced, I might say, and by a horse! Let's go!'

'Go?' echoed Hattie.

'Yes, go,' repeated Alicia, reaching for an old, moth-eaten fur coat that hung on the back door peg along with a pom-pom hat. 'We need to denounce this imposter.'

'Denounce?' echoed Hattie. Perhaps A.C. Hennessy was really loopy. First of all talking about rescue, and then saying they must go.

'Denounce,' said Alicia, whose voice had now grown deep and strong. 'Accuse, challenge, inform against . . . Don't you have a dictionary at Hubert & Busters?'

'Yes, but . . .' said Hattie.

'Well then, *we must arise now and go to*

161

Innisfree,' said Alicia.

'Innisfree?' repeated Hattie (*Batty*, she was thinking. *That's what Mr Gadly had called her, and obviously he was right.*)

'I mean *Dizzy Perch*,' said Alicia. 'I trust you have some sort of a vehicle?'

'Well, yes,' said Hattie. 'I've a motorbike.'

'A motorbike? Ah! My dear Charles Heathcliffe had one of those. Would I be right in thinking I need a helmet?'

'You would,' said Hattie.

'Wait! Stand by!' cried Alicia, and disappeared into what looked like a broom cupboard, reappearing with a dusty helmet and an equally dusty pair of goggles. Alicia wiped the dust off the helmet. Hattie saw a picture of a winged face on the front. *Knight Rider*, she read.

Alicia giggled. 'Charles Heathcliffe,' she said. 'He had a way with words too. Are we ready? I feel we must waste no time in confronting this pretender.'

Outside Garden Cottage they both put on their goggles and helmets.

'Now I'm your double,' said Alicia.

'You'll have to hold tight to me,' said Hattie, 'particularly going round corners.'

'Happily, happily,' said Alicia. 'What a fine day it is.'

'I'm not entirely sure of the way,' said Hattie. 'But I know it's quite a long way to Scotland.'

'Just put your foot down,' said Alicia. 'Isn't that the way?'

'Yes,' said Hattie, and did.

They were soon roaring through towns and villages. Alicia seemed to be singing, but Hattie couldn't hear the words over the noise of the engine.

But they hadn't gone more than ten miles when Alicia shouted, 'Stop! Stop!'

Hattie managed to pull in to a lay-by. *She's changed her mind*, she thought. *She wants to go home*. 'What is it?' she asked.

'I've remembered,' said Alicia, taking off her helmet and goggles as if to hold her face up to the sun and stretch her arms out to the world.

'Remembered what?' asked Hattie. She

hoped they wouldn't have to go back so that Alicia could turn off the gas or the tap she'd left running.

'Remembered what I wanted to be rescued from,' said Alicia triumphantly.

'And it was . . . ?' asked Hattie.

'Why, myself, of course,' said Alicia. 'I wanted to be rescued from myself. And now I haven't thought of myself for at least ten miles. Instead I'm off on this grand adventure to rescue someone else! Thank you, my dear!'

'It's a pleasure,' said Hattie. And meant it. 'But we've still a long way to go.'

'Foot down,' said Alicia.

'Foot down,' repeated Hattie and off they roared again.

It was dusk when Moll and Ma reached Big Mac's field. Moll slid off Amber's back. Ma, still hanging on to Amber's mane for dear life, opened her eyes.

'Dear Thing, where are we?' she asked in a rather shaky voice.

'Well, well, well! Blow me down with a feather if it isn't Maisie Elizabeth Ann Coggin!' roared a voice that was horribly familiar. 'Hang it all, Moll, you've excelled yourself. I send you out to catch a tiddler and you come home with a big fat trout!' Big Mac was bent double with laughter, slapping his thighs and pointing a disbelieving finger at Ma.

Ma struggled inelegantly off Amber's back, and glared at Big Mac.

'As I live and breathe, if it isn't you, Big Mac Malone!' said Ma. 'And who would you be calling a trout?' And before either Moll or Big Mac could do anything to stop her, she'd stretched up and boxed Big Mac's ears.

Big Mac howled with rage. 'I'll tell you this, woman,' he shouted, 'if you'd married me instead of that . . . that nincompoop, Amos flipping Coggin, you'd not be left alone living in a crazy house with too many children and too many books.'

'Only three children,' said Ma, 'and not nearly enough books.' Ma turned to Moll. 'Ace,

Dear Thing,' she said. 'I imagine this was the only place you could find to provide Amber with a good stable, but I'm sure you've got enough material for your next book now, so if you wouldn't mind I'd like to stop being a heroine and ask you, no *insist*, that you take me back to *Dizzy Perch* at once.'

'I'm terribly sorry, Ma,' said Moll, 'I can't do that, because you see I'm not really Ace.'

'Not really A.C. Hennessy?' asked Ma, turning pale. 'I don't understand.' Ma sank down on a tree stump. She looked suddenly much smaller.

Big Mac crouched down, so he could glower at her. Ma saw that his ears were burning from where she'd boxed them, his face was purply-red with temper, and his eyes were slits of nastiness.

'Oh, hoity-toity, take me home to *Dizzy Perch* at once! There's an awful lot you don't understand Maisie Elizabeth Ann Coggin. That you never understood. That you didn't understand when you turned me down. That you didn't understand when Amos flipping Coggin went off with all the prizes at school and university, using all my ideas, all my research . . .'

'I really don't think so . . .' began Ma, trying to stand up, only her legs felt jellyish so she sat down again rather quickly.

'You don't think so?' crowed Big Mac. 'You just never think! I've heard all about you from Moll here . . .'

Oh dear, thought Moll. She'd hoped some memory of romance would have softened Big Mac's heart, even that he might give up his scheme of revenge. Should she have told Ma, before carrying her off? Would she have come?

'Moll?' queried Ma, looking totally confused.

'*I'm* Moll,' said Moll. 'And I'm very sorry, Ma, but you've been kidnapped.'

'Kidnapped?' squeaked Ma.

'Better call it Ma-napped!' said Big Mac, and roared with laughter.

'I'd better explain,' said Moll.

Chapter 14

A Very Long Night

Up in *Dizzy Perch* they set a light in every window until the house shone in the dark almost as if it had turned itself into a lighthouse. A few gulls, up late, flew round it in a puzzled kind of way. The house shone so brightly that Mrs Tansley in the Post Office Stores could see it from her bedroom window.

'I suppose they're having a party,' she said crossly, and drew her curtains.

Titch and Lottie were snuggled up together in Titch's bed. Titch had cried himself to sleep. Grandpa and Oliver, both of them wrapped in blankets, sat out on Grandpa's balcony. 'You and I will keep watch,' Grandpa said. He'd found an old searchlight. They took it in turns to sweep the beach with light. The tide was just on the turn. The sea wore its darkest, deepest look. It grew chilly. The sky darkened as if to match the sea. Grandpa fetched a rug and spread it across their knees.

Slowly, as they sat there, watching and waiting, Oliver told Grandpa all about the visit to the library in Brochmuir and how he and Cezary had looked up A.C. Hennessy in a book called *Who's Who* and how a very nice girl called Emily had told them she was a recluse.

'*Who's Who* said she was "passionate about her privacy",' said Oliver. 'And Emily said that was the same as being a recluse.'

'Why on earth didn't you come and tell me?' said Grandpa. 'Me or Ma, or both of us?' The lateness and strangeness of the night meant they were both speaking quietly. In his sleep, Titch heard the drone of their voices and was vaguely comforted.

'I didn't think anyone would believe me,' said Oliver. 'Everyone loved Ace and Amber.

You'd all just have been angry with me.'

Grandpa put an arm round Oliver's shoulders. 'I'm afraid you're probably right,' he said. 'Ace – or whoever she is – had us all in a kind of enchantment. So what did you do?'

'Cezary and I went to Brochmuir on the bus. On the way back, we told Stan all about Ace being an imposter and Stan suggested we write a letter to the real A.C. Hennessy. We had the address of her publishers, you see. Stan said we could write to Miss Hennessy *care of Hubert and Busters*. So that's what we did. Me and Cezary.'

'And . . . ?' said Grandpa.

'And we're waiting,' said Oliver, 'hoping she might reply. Before Ace – or whoever she is – took off with Ma, I was going to go this afternoon to the Post Office Stores to see if there was a reply.'

'Even if there is,' said Grandpa, 'it might be too late now.'

'No,' said Oliver. 'Stan bet us three bags of chips and a bottle of lemonade that the real

Miss Hennessy would do something about it.'

'I can't think what,' said Grandpa gloomily.

In the field at the edge of Starwater, the only creature asleep was Amber. Big Mac raged about his caravan. This wasn't easy. There wasn't enough space for a truly good rage of the stamping kind which was Big Mac's preference.

'Women! Sisters! Coggins!' stamped Big Mac. He'd been all for tying Maisie Elizabeth Ann up, and tweaking her nose until she told him where Amos flipping Coggin was. But Moll had told him she'd never cook him another supper if he did that, and Maisie had told him it would be a waste of time anyway because she didn't know where Pa was.

'Not know!' screeched Big Mac. 'Not know!'

'Amos thought it was best if I didn't know,' said Ma. 'Safer. And he was right. The only person who knows is Oliver.'

And then Ma clapped a hand over her mouth.

'Oliver!' growled Big Mac. 'Well, Moll, I'm

just going to add a nice little P.S. to the ransom note, and you can take it to *Dizzy Perch*.'

'No,' said Moll. 'I won't. I won't do it. You can take it yourself!'

'It's dark!' howled Big Mac.

'Tough!' said Moll. 'I need a pillow and some blankets for Ma.'

'She can sleep in the field for all I care,' said Big Mac.

But, threatened with another box on the ears, he flung out one tatty pillow and a couple of old blankets. Then he slammed the caravan door, tore up his first ransom note and wrote another. This one read:

IF YOU WANT YOUR MA BACK
UNHARMED
REVEAL ADDRESS OF
COGGIN (PROF)
LEAVE SAME
AT POST OFFICE STORES
STARWATER
SOONEST

After some thought, he signed it 'Anon'.

Then he took out his telescope and focused it on *Dizzy Perch*. *Dizzy Perch*, all lit up. 'Like a flipping Christmas tree,' Big Mac said to himself, and groaned. He groaned again when he saw the tide was on the turn. Still too full in for him to go along the beach. It meant he'd have to go over the rocks in the dark. He put on his thickest jumper, with a cagoul on top, pulled the hood up tight and wound an old scarf round his neck. But first he had to get to Starwater. His old jalopy hadn't been used since he'd parked the caravan in the field some three months ago. At least it would save him a five-mile walk to the village.

He was so bundled up in clothes that he had to squeeze himself into the car, and then, because it had sat idle for so long, it took him an age, and a lot of noise, to get the engine going. Big Mac revved the noise up as loud as he could, just to annoy Moll. Then he gave a quick *So There!* toot. That would let them know he meant business, he thought.

Up in the hayloft Moll found an old pair of pyjamas for Ma.

Ma, who wasn't at all grateful. Ma, who could hardly decide if she was very angry or very upset or both. Ma, who sat bolt upright in Moll's bed (while Moll, sacrificing her own bed, gathered the few thin blankets about herself), saying over and over again in an awful wailing voice, first, 'How could you do it? How could you do it?' and then, 'How could I have been so foolish?'

Moll couldn't answer the second question, but tried to answer the first. She tried to tell Ma all about Big Mac's threats, how their father had left money to Big Mac and Amber to her, and how she simply couldn't bear to think of Amber being starved to death.

'I was really hoping there'd be some way I could persuade Big Mac to give up his idea of getting revenge, of Pa being his Sworn Enemy,' Moll said. 'Big Mac has always had obsessions of one sort or another. Usually they wear themselves out, like a jersey that's in shreds

174

because it's been worn every day. Only somehow he's kept this one going. Maybe if you'd been kinder to him, flattered him a little?' she suggested.

But at this Ma looked as if she was considering boxing Moll's ears too.

Both of them went very quiet when they heard Big Mac drive out of the field, the old jalopy bumping over the ruts and dips before giving its final rude toot and making Amber neigh in alarm.

'He's taking the ransom note,' said Moll. 'I didn't think he'd have the nerve. He wants the address for Pa – for Professor Coggin – in return for you.'

'I'm not altogether sure they'll want me back,' said Ma, and had a little weep, thinking of all her Dear Things being without her, and missing a goodnight kiss.

'Try to sleep,' said Moll.

'I can't possibly sleep without a story,' said Ma.

'Oh,' groaned Moll to herself, 'why on earth

didn't I think to bring a book?'

'You'll have to make one up,' said Ma.

And so for the rest of the night, Moll told Ma story after story after story.

And eventually, just before Ma at last fell asleep, she said, 'You should write those down.'

Yes, thought Moll. *I jolly well might.*

Hattie and Alicia had a very good night's sleep. They had driven half the way to Scotland when Hattie said she didn't think she could drive any further that night, and anyway, she needed petrol.

'We shall stay somewhere grand,' said Alicia. 'Now that I'm rescued I plan to enjoy myself.'

'I don't know about somewhere grand,' said Hattie. 'We can try and find a small B & B. Somewhere cheap.'

'But I have plenty of money,' said Alicia, producing a fat wallet from the pocket of her fur coat. 'Hubert & Busters pay me quite well, you know.'

So that was how they ended up in the Royal

Balmoral Hotel which Hattie remembered all her life and told her grandchildren about because it was the grandest hotel she'd ever been in and the bed made her feel just like a princess. Furthermore, when Alicia had signed the hotel register, the man at the reception desk had been very impressed.

'Not *the* A.C. Hennessy?' he said.

And Alicia had said 'The very same,' as if she had got quite used to being famous.

Up at *Dizzy Perch*, Oliver and Grandpa tried to take it in turns to keep watch. But by about four o'clock both of them had nodded off. So they didn't see Big Mac struggling down the rocks, puffing and panting as he clambered down on to the beach and found the gate and the bell that rang for the funicular. He threw the ransom note on the chair of the funicular and danged the bell as hard as he could. Then, out of breath as he was, he stumbled away along the thin line of beach left as the tide slowly began its retreat.

The bell echoed through the house. 'It's the

funicular!' said Oliver, startling awake and shaking Grandpa. 'There's someone down there! Perhaps it's Ma coming home.'

And without waiting for Grandpa, he ran to wind up the funicular. Grandpa, still tousled with sleep, was soon behind him.

'There can't be anyone there,' said Oliver desperately, 'it feels far too light.'

It was Grandpa who took the ransom note from the empty chair. They read it together.

'I'm afraid you'll have to tell this person what they want to know,' said Grandpa, putting his arm round Oliver. 'If you want your Ma back that is.'

For all of one second Oliver considered *not* getting Ma back. This was all her fault, wasn't it? Then with a kind of sob that he turned into a hiccup, he said, 'Yes, I'll do it. I'll take Pa's address to the Post Office Stores.'

So that was how it came about, that early on Sunday morning – when the tide was rolled far back against the sky, and while Grandpa was trying to coax Titch and Lottie to have some breakfast – Oliver, with the address of Pa's laboratory in Auchterlaldy, was running along the beach to Starwater, shaking his fist at whoever it was who'd kidnapped his Ma and wanted to harm his Pa.

At about the same hour, Big Mac was lurking in his car by the harbour wall, keeping an eye on the Post Office Stores, watching to see which of the Coggins appeared with the answer to his ransom note.

And round about the same hour, Hattie and Alicia, having had the hugest breakfast ever, were just a few miles away from the Post Office Stores.

Mrs Tansley, who only opened the Stores on Sunday for the newspapers, rolled up the blind and looked out at a nice spring morning.

As for Moll and Ma, they were still fast asleep.

Chapter 15

The Famous Anon

Mrs Tansley couldn't quite believe what was going on. It being Sunday morning, she had her hair in rollers, a scarf wound round like a turban. Also, she hadn't put her lipstick on and suddenly there was a rush of people in the Stores, and none of them apparently wanting newspapers.

First in was the Coggin boy, Oliver. Mrs Tansley had grown quite fond of Oliver over the last couple of years. Often, she and Mr Strut, the postman, discussed the strangeness of *Dizzy Perch* and the family who lived there. Why, Mrs Tansley asked Mr Strut, was it always that poor boy who did all the shopping, and who most of the time looked as if he'd grown out of

his clothes and needed . . . well, a good hug?
Did he not have a mother? A father? And Mr
Strut said wisely that he didn't know, and
further that nothing, absolutely nothing, would
make him climb the cliffs or walk all along the
beach to deliver letters to *Dizzy Perch*. Mrs
Tansley, who privately thought Strut was a bit
lazy, but didn't want to lose him, said, well, that
didn't matter, because there never *were* any
letters for *Dizzy Perch*.

That Sunday morning Mrs Tansley thought
Oliver looked even more in need of a hug
than usual.

'Tear-stained,' she told Mr Strut the following
day. 'And when he'd last seen a comb, I don't
know. Looked as if he'd slept in his clothes.' But
of course that hadn't been the strangest thing.
'First thing, he asks if there's any letter for him
and I had to say no. He looked so disappointed.
His face fell as if he'd just had very bad news.
Then he handed me a letter of his own, as if he
didn't want to but somehow *had to*. Well, it
wasn't a proper letter.'

'What d'you mean, not a proper letter?' asked Mr Strut.

'No address. Just a rather tatty envelope with "TO ANON" written on it. "Who's this for?" I asked—'

'Well, that was a rather silly question,' Mr Strut had said, glad of an opportunity to get one up on Mrs T.

'I suppose it was,' said Mrs Tansley. 'But I couldn't help myself and he – Oliver – just said, "It'll be collected". "By who?" I asked.'

'Another silly question,' said Mr Strut. 'I suppose you didn't look inside? I mean, being postmistress, one could say you had a duty . . .'

'Well,' said Mrs Tansley, patting her turbaned rollers, 'it wasn't exactly sealed. And as you say, I have a certain duty . . .'

'And . . . ?' asked Mr Strut, straining to look over the counter, to see if *TO ANON* was still there. (It wasn't.)

'Well, there was just an address,' said Mrs Tansley. 'And not much of one at that. It was

The Laboratory, Near Loch Wardle, Auchterlaldy. Something like that.'

'"Something like that"? You mean you didn't write it down? Mrs T, sometimes I think you have a very small brain.'

Mrs Tansley had taken the huff at that, and told him he'd better get on with his round, and then regretted it because she would very much like to have told him what happened next.

Which was that soon after Oliver had left, looking sadder than she'd ever seen him look, a *huge* man dressed all in black strode into the Stores, just like a cowboy from one of those Westerns. He took a bottle of Irn Bru off the shelf, opened it with his teeth, and drank it down in one. (In bed that night, Mrs Tansley improvised the story she would have told Mr Strut if she hadn't sent him off on his round.) *And then*, she continued in her imaginary conversation with Mr Strut, *he demanded to know if* that boy *had left him a message*.

With a shaking hand she'd given him the envelope addressed to *TO ANON*. 'Sunday

Dispatch?' she'd offered weakly, waving the newspaper at his departing back. But he made no answer, simply strode off, leaving the Stores' doorbell tingling behind him and her heart jingling so fast she'd had to sit down on a stool behind the counter and pat all her rollers to make sure they hadn't come adrift.

Hardly had she recovered when a motorbike roared up and two helmeted figures burst in – *like bank robbers*, was how she planned to tell Mr Strut – one of them in a fur coat, the other in what-you-call-'em, leathers. The younger of the two had thrown back her helmet and taken off her goggles. The older one had spotted the newspapers, picked one up and seemed as if she was about to sit down and read it.

'Has a boy been here?' said the young motorbike rider. 'And would he happen to be called Oliver?'

'Well, yes he would,' said Mrs Tansley. 'And a nicer boy you couldn't find, only not much looked after in my opinion. He left a message for someone.'

'Who?' asked both Mrs Tansley's customers.

'I'm afraid I can't really tell you that,' said Mrs Tansley. 'It was addressed "To Anon"!'

'Ah! The famous Anon!' cried the fur-coated rider, dropping the newspaper she'd been reading on the floor in a crumpled heap so that Mrs Tansley glowered at her.

'I'm glad you know all about the famous Anon,' said Mrs Tansley stiffly, 'but I can't say I do. Or want to,' she added. 'But there was a man in here just five minutes ago who picked up the message, so maybe he's the famous Anon.'

Hattie picked up the crumpled newspaper, smoothed it down, laid it carefully on the rack with the other papers and gave Mrs Tansley her very best smile.

'I suppose you don't happen to know where this . . . this particular famous Anon was going, do you?' she asked.

Mrs Tansley pushed her spectacles up her nose, patted her turban again and said, 'Well, confidentially . . .'

'Confidentially . . .' echoed Hattie.

'Mention was made of a place called Auchterlaldy . . .'

Hardly were the words out of her mouth when the two riders clamped their helmets back on and were off. Mrs Tansley heard them roaring out of Starwater.

'Loud enough to waken the dead,[she said.

Oliver walked miserably to the harbour. Sometimes just looking at the boats, seeing the fishermen mending their nets, watching the gulls beaking up leftovers made him feel better. It was the whole orderly, regular routine of it all.

On a Sunday morning it was quiet. There was nothing for it but to go back home. Was home *home* without Ma? And how long would it be before whoever it was who'd written that note, got to Pa's laboratory? The only thing he'd left out of the address was that there was only a narrow, rough track to Auchterlaldy, and not a signpost in sight. Might the writer of the ransom note get lost? Forever! That was his only hope. If not, if he got to the laboratory, what might he do to Pa? Maybe neither Ma nor Pa would ever come back to *Dizzy Perch*. He'd be an orphan with just Grandpa, Titch and Lottie to look after. And what would they live *on*?

Oliver brushed the tears away. This wouldn't help anyone. They'd all be waiting for him up at *Dizzy Perch*. Oliver had turned towards the Creel Road when a bounding, wagging, black-and-white dog came jumping up at him.

'Cheerio!' cried Oliver, allowing himself to be thoroughly licked. And behind Cheerio came Cezary, running down from Seaview Terrace and giving Oliver the hug that Mrs Tansley had wanted to give him.

'What's happened? You look terrible,' said Cezary. 'As if you've lost a pound and found a penny. You come and tell me.'

So Oliver did. Sitting on the blue bench outside 3 Seaview Terrace, where the boys had often sat exchanging news with Cheerio lying across their feet. He told him how Ace had ridden off with Ma on the back of Amber . . .

'She kidnap her!' gasped Cezary.

'Yes. And then we waited all night – Grandpa, Lottie, Titch, and me – and this morning there was this ransom note.'

'What it want? What it say?' asked Cezary.

Oliver had to swallow hard before he could answer. 'Pa's address,' he said.

'You no give him,' said Cezary.

'I don't have any choice,' said Oliver. 'If I want Ma home.'

'That is terrible bargain,' said Cezary. 'That is blackmail.'

'Yes,' said Oliver, so miserably that Cheerio put his paws on Oliver's knees and gave him several extra licks. 'I expect he's on the way to Auchterlaldy now. Maybe he'll kidnap Pa too. Or worse . . .' Oliver didn't like to say what might be worse.

'We have no words from real Hennessy?'

'Nothing,' said Oliver.

'Well, then,' said Cezary, jumping to his feet, straightening his shoulders and looking ready to take on the world. 'We must do this ourselves. This kidnapper must be stopped. We go to your Pa's rescue.'

'I wish,' said Oliver, his voice low with despair. 'But how?'

'Stan!' said Cezary.

Chapter 16

A Race

All of a sudden the road to Loch Wardle – usually almost empty on a Sunday – was very busy.

First off was Big Mac. As soon as he'd torn open the envelope from Oliver and seen the address, he'd driven back to Moll and Ma, and without turning off the engine, shouted up to them in the hayloft. Amber whinnied alarm and kicked at her stable door. Moll and Ma looked out of the small wooden hatch that served as a window.

'Maisie Elizabeth Ann Coggin! Get yourself down here!' shouted Big Mac. 'I know where that Amos flipping Coggin is and I'm off to get him. His time's up. I'm going to claim what's mine. By this time tomorrow I'll be a wealthy man. Now get yourself down here!'

'We're not going anywhere!' shouted Ma.

Big Mac flung his arms wide and addressed the sky. 'Oh ho, ho,' he cried, 'the lady says she's not going nowhere. Maybe she doesn't care if she don't see her kiddies again! Maybe she doesn't care a bit what happens to that precious Amos flipping Coggin. Maybe she's just going to stay here for ever and ever.'

By the time he'd finished speaking, Ma – red in the face, rumpled, crumpled, and cross – was down by the car.

'I'm not coming!' shouted Moll. 'I'm not doing what you want me to do ever again!'

'Who cares?' shouted Big Mac. 'You're no more use to me. You get in,' he said to Ma and pushed her, scowling, into the back seat. 'I reckon that Amos Coggin will do whatever I want him to do when he sees who I've got sitting in the back seat.'

And, revving the car up, they bounced out of the bumpy field and on to the road to Loch Wardle.

* * *

Hattie and Alicia had to stop at Brochmuir to find a map. And even when they'd bought one and Hattie had parked in a lay-by so they could study it, it took them ages to spot Auchterlaldy, which was marked with so small a spot you'd think the mapmaker didn't want anyone to find the place.

'It's near Loch Wardle,' said Hattie. 'But I'm not sure there's even a road to Auchterlaldy.'

'I suppose a map tells a story,' said Alicia, 'in a way. But I do prefer words.'

'There's plenty of words,' said Hattie a little crossly. 'Place names. And I'd be very grateful if you could follow the map while I drive.'

'I'll try,' said Alicia. 'I'll rest the map against your back and then maybe I can see where we are going. How fast can this machine go?'

'A hundred miles per hour,' said Hattie, settling her helmet back on.

'Go for it!' cried Alicia.

* * *

Bus Number X254 was parked in its usual place, at the top of the hill leading down to Starwater. But on Sunday there was no Stan. Sunday was the bus and Stan's day off.

'He lives in one of the cottages behind the harbour,' said Cezary. 'I've seen him go there at night.'

In an urgent gabble, Cezary had explained to his parents that he and Oliver needed to go and rescue Oliver's father. And though his mother looked very anxious, Cezary's father patted him on the shoulder and said, 'You must do what you have to do. I trust you.' And Cezary's mother had produced biscuits and two bottles of lemonade. 'For the journey,' she said.

Then they were running round the harbour and banging on Stan's door, both of them almost too breathless to speak.

Almost before Oliver had finished gasping out his story about Ma being kidnapped and having to take the ransom note to the Post Office Stores, Stan was reaching for the keys to the bus and all three of them were running up the hill.

'Hey!' someone shouted behind them. 'I thought the bus didn't go on a Sunday?'

'It doesn't,' shouted Stan. 'This is an emergency!'

Oliver wished X254 knew this. He thought the bus would never start up. And when it did, it was with such a worrying rattle it was difficult to believe it would keep going. 'We'll probably end up pushing it,' he said to Cezary.

'Not when there's just the three of us aboard,' said Stan. 'This old lady has never let me down yet.'

'Old lady?' asked Cezary.

'He means the bus,' said Oliver.

So then there were three lots of people on the road to Auchterlaldy and if anyone should happen to be watching, it would be hard to guess who would get there first.

Big Mac had been first to leave Starwater, but his car was old and he had to keep stopping because first Ma said she was going to be sick and then she said she needed a pee, and then he took two wrong turnings because Ma kept telling him he was a rogue and a rascal and a bandit and a baddie and a no-good nobody.

Hattie and Hennessy had the fastest vehicle, of course but Alicia proved no good at reading a map at all and in fact at one rather fast corner the map flew away altogether and they had to stop and turn back and find it, rather muddy, in a hedge.

Stan and the boys were last to leave Starwater, and even though Stan made the bus go as fast as it could (which was just about forty miles an hour), they were slow. But Stan was the only one who really knew the way. Every day except Sundays, he'd been driving to Loch Wardle for years and years and years.

And Stan and Oliver were the only ones who knew that, as Hattie had suspected, there wasn't a road to Auchterlaldy. So the only way to Pa's laboratory was on foot. Which meant anyone might get there first.

There was one person who was *not* on the road to Aucherlaldy. Moll.

'This might be our last ride to *Dizzy Perch*,' Moll told Amber as they galloped along the beach.

Grandpa, Lottie and Titch were all out on Grandpa's balcony when they arrived.

'Where's my Ma?' shouted Titch.

'Why are you so lovely outside and so nasty inside?' shouted Lottie.

'You're never coming in again!' shouted Titch.

'I have to agree,' said Grandpa.

Moll tied Amber up as she usually did, found a stick, and in big letters on the sand she wrote *I AM VERY SORRY*.

But it didn't seem to help. Titch and Lottie just threw old apples down on her head. Amber was very grateful.

Chapter 17

They're Behind You

Hattie and Hennessy should have been first at the Laboratory. Hattie's Harley Davidson went twice as fast as Big Mac's old jalopy and probably three times as fast as Stan's bus. Indeed, Oliver and Cezary saw the bikers ride past them not once, but twice.

'Not seen that one on this road before,' said Stan.

'Maybe that's the kidnapper,' said Oliver. 'Can't you go any faster?'

'Sorry, lad,' said Stan. 'I don't think it's your kidnapper or your imposter. Looked like a young girl and an old woman to me. The old one's wearing a fur coat. Bit odd in spring.'

'That could be a disguise!' said Oliver, jiggling up and down in his seat.

Stan laid a reassuring hand on his shoulder. 'Just stay calm, lad. Remember, you know the way up to Auchterlaldy and, apart from your Pa, no one else does,' he said.

Oliver sat back and tried to relax, remembering the first time Stan had brought him up to the Highlands. That was when Pa hadn't come home when he said he would and they'd all thought something awful had happened to him – only it hadn't, he'd just been so caught up in his work that he'd forgotten. Oliver had borrowed the last of the housekeeping money for the bus fare. But then, Bus Number X254 had been full of passengers and all of them, it seemed, friends of Stan. That day, when they reached Loch Wardle – the final stop on Stan's route – Oliver had been the last one on the bus.

Stan had produced cake and lemonade and two canvas stools, and the two of them had sat by the loch while Oliver had talked about *Dizzy*

198

Perch and Pa's important secret work, and how worried they were about him, and how Titch was poorly and Ma was lovelorn and Grandpa was very old and, last but not least, they'd run out of money. So that was why he, Oliver, had to come and find him.

'There's something about the oldest son,' Stan had said. 'Always has to take charge in the end.' Oliver remembered this now. It had given him courage then. He needed it now. Next to Cezary, Stan had become Oliver's best friend.

Oliver had kept the map he'd found in the chest in Pa's study. Cezary was studying it. With his finger he followed the wiggly line Pa had drawn and that ran along the coast almost to the top of the map and then turned off to reach a tiny dot. Auchterlaldy

'It doesn't look easy to find,' said Cezary.

'It isn't,' said Stan and Oliver together.

The reason the bus had been twice overtaken by Hattie and Hennessy was that Hennessy kept forgetting where they were going and why.

'This is such a wonderful journey,' Alicia shouted in Hattie's helmeted ear. 'Can we just stop to look at that view? Why on earth have I stayed at home so long? Let's stop, just for a moment! Please!'

And Hattie, who was a kindly girl, stopped the bike and they both got off and looked at the lochs that lay still and mysterious beneath them. Stan could have told them that they were going through the Great Glen, made by glaciers millions of years ago.

And then, somehow, there were a lot of stops. Alicia seemed to think she was on holiday – which, in a way, she was. So if it wasn't the view it was a stunning waterfall or a whole glade of bluebells. 'Marvellous! Marvellous!' Alicia said. 'I'm having a marvellous time.'

'Actually, we are trying to find Oliver and rescue his father from an imposter,' Hattie reminded her.

Alicia looked quite surprised. 'Rescue,' she said. 'Oh yes, I know all about rescue,' and obediently got back on the motorbike, and off they roared, overtaking the bus for the second time and an old jalopy that tooted at them.

Even so, it was Big Mac in the old jalopy who reached Loch Wardle first, Hattie and Hennessy having at least another four urgent sightseeing halts, and Stan's bus not capable of going faster than forty miles an hour.

Big Mac had stopped at the one and only pub on the road – making sure the car doors were locked – and was given directions to Loch Wardle which included a shortcut.

'You don't want to go to Auchterlaldy,' the publican said. 'There's nothing and nobody there. Used to be an old shepherd, but I think he's long gone.'

An old shepherd, thought Big Mac. Sworn Enemy was cunning enough to disguise himself as an old shepherd. He got back in the car and drove on.

In the back of the car, Ma had given up calling him names – 'squawking like an old hen', as Big Mac told her – and had at last fallen asleep. She woke up as Big Mac brought the car to a sudden halt.

'Where are we? Where are we?' Ma shouted, pummelling Big Mac on the back, which he took as if her fists were the taps of a baby.

'This is Loch Wardle,' said Big Mac. 'And a godforsaken place if ever there was one.'

Ma looked out of the window and shivered. The smallest of the lochs, it was surrounded by tall pine trees that seemed to have gathered themselves together almost like a legion of soldiers. What sunshine there was, was blocked out by the trees. A sort of gauzy mist lingered over the loch and hung above the trees, as if this was a place no one ever came. As if spring couldn't get a look in here. As if, in the absence of people, the place was growing some kind of spirit of its own.

Big Mac stomped about a bit, telling himself not to be foolish. It was typical of Sworn Enemy to find some place like this just to make Big Mac's life difficult. But Auchterlaldy? Which way was that? The road itself had stopped.

There was just a steep track going the Lord knew where.

Big Mac wished he'd brought his telescope. He was just wondering whether to backtrack a bit, see if there was another, more passable road to Auchterlaldy, when he spotted a rough wooden signpost that said *Auchterlaldy* in faded ink. And when he looked carefully, he saw faint rings of smoke drifting up to the sky. So this was it, Big Mac said to himself, Sworn Enemy's laboratory. At last!

He parked the car where it was half hidden under a swag of ivy.

'Out you get,' he said to Ma, 'it's time you were useful. We're going up there.'

Ma looked up the track. 'Up there?' she said weakly.

'To the top!' said Big Mac. 'To your beloved,' he added, with a grin that was more snarl than smile.

'My legs,' said Ma, 'are not that good.'

'That's because you haven't used 'em enough,' said Big Mac. 'Now's your chance.'

'Can't we just call him down?' asked Ma.

Big Mac didn't bother to answer. He gave her a push that sent her tottering up the first part of the track.

Big Mac's legs were – well – big. But much like Ma, he wasn't used to exercise. He was soon very short of puff, and almost glad Ma was so slow that he had to stop and wait for her.

The track wound up and up until even the trees seemed to give up. There was nothing but scrub, rough grass, stones, sky and even smaller tracks that led nowhere. They passed an almost derelict cottage, its stones gathering moss, its roof fallen in. There was a turning just past it. Squinting up towards the smoke, the sun flickering through the trees in a way that dazzled him, Big Mac reckoned this was the way. He pushed Ma onwards.

'I must have a bit of a rest,' panted Ma. 'My legs are in ribbons with all this scratchy stuff, and both my heels have got blisters.'

'Tough,' said Big Mac, but he too was glad of

a rest. After all, he'd waited this long to confront Sworn Enemy. What did another five or ten minutes matter?

They mattered enough for Hattie and Alicia to catch them up.

As Big Mac had done, Hattie gazed up the track, saw the signpost saying *Auchterlaldy* and spotted the smoke.

'I can't drive up there,' she said to Alicia. 'We'll have to walk.'

'Lovely!' said Alicia. 'And what a wonderful place! This little hidden loch.'

'Not a bit spooky?' asked Hattie.

'Magical,' said Alicia. 'Magical and mysterious. I must make a note.'

Alicia took a five pound note out of her wallet, together with a stub of pencil, and began writing on it. 'For a future story,' she said.

'We really haven't time for that,' said Hattie. 'Come on. D'you think you can climb up there?'

(Alicia was so skinny she didn't look as if she'd walked anywhere, ever.)

'Oh yes,' Alicia answered. 'I'll just dump my coat down here.' And she tossed the fur over the bike which Hattie had propped against a withered tree stump.

The pair began to climb.

Big Mac heard their voices coming towards him, echoing up the empty track.

A deep voice saying, 'I expect the view will be fantastic.'

A lighter voice saying, 'Do come on. We're not here for the view. This is serious.'

'What the . . . ?' began Big Mac. 'Who is it?'

Hattie and Alicia were still too far down the track for him to see them. 'D'you recognise the voices?' Big Mac asked.

'No,' said Ma. 'I don't.'

'It could be someone else after the vaccine,' said Big Mac, beginning to sweat. 'Whoever it is, said "serious". I can't be beaten at this stage.'

Big Mac scrambled to his feet and pulled Ma up on hers.

'Get going,' he said. 'I've got to be first.'

Which is how Hattie spotted two rather large bottoms up ahead of them.

'I think that might be the imposter up ahead,' said Hattie nervously. 'At least one of them might be. The other one looks . . . well, scary.'

'This is more exciting than any story I've ever written,' said Alicia.

'Oh do shut up,' said Hattie.

'I can hear a strange rattly noise,' said Alicia. 'D'you think some ancient creatures live round here?'

'No,' said Hattie looking back down the track. 'It looks like a very old bus. Keep going.'

The bus did more than just rattle. It rattled and shuddered. Shuddered and rattled, gave a last splutter, and stopped.

'Made it!' said Stan but the boys were already out of the bus and at the bottom of the track.

'Come with us!' Oliver shouted to Stan.

'You'll be faster without me,' Stan called back. 'I'll be here if you need me.'

Will we, wondered Oliver, with a kind of shiver of dread, *need him?*

'It's this way,' he said to Cezary. 'Up here. Quite a long way.'

But Cezary was already ahead of him. Running up the track as if his life depended on it.

'Is your Pa crazy?' he called back over his shoulder.

Stan watched them go. He was about to climb back into the bus and perhaps have a sandwich or two when he saw it. A large furry animal. It looked as if it was asleep.

Stan picked up a long stick and very slowly crept up on it. He poked at it. It didn't move. Stan crept closer. Poked the stick more fiercely. Up leapt the furry animal! Stan fell backwards with Alicia's fur coat on top of him.

Chapter 18

Pa

'The thing you need to know about Amos Coggin,' Ma panted, 'is that he's very, very bright and very, very foolish.'

Since hearing voices behind them, Big Mac had put on a spurt. He'd been forced to hold Ma's hand so that she could keep up.

'What are you talking about, woman?' he said. 'Amos Coggin? One of the great brains of the country? Foolish? It's you that's foolish. More than foolish. Daft!' And he yanked her up a particularly bumpy part of the track.

Ma hadn't breath enough to do more than sigh. When the laboratory was in sight, Big Mac produced a length of rope and tied Ma to him.

'Like a little puppy on a lead,' he said and chucked her under the chin. Ma glowered at him.

Up in his Highland eyrie, Pa – he of the great brain (according to Big Mac), and both very bright and very foolish (according to Ma) – was feeling very sorry for himself.

Two weeks ago he had sent his old friend Joe off, by helicopter, with the precious samples of the life-saving vaccine, to the chemistry department of Orlachan University. Of course there was more work to be done. The vaccine would have to undergo tests. The tests might take years. On the table lay several letters that he'd received while at *Dizzy Perch* from various drugs companies, offering large sums of money for his results. He hadn't replied. He had to be absolutely certain that the vaccine wouldn't be misused. There was talk of warlords, presidents, generals all too willing to release terrible chemical sprays, the equivalent of poisonous gas, in order to quell rebellions. He knew that

Professor Ruairidh Gordon at Orlachan University could be completely trusted.

But this wasn't what was making him sorry for himself. Sorry for himself and sad. It was a beautiful day. Almost the start of summer, Pa noticed, as he opened the door of the laboratory and stood for a few moments breathing in the air. Soon he wouldn't need his wood-burning stove, he thought, though up here there was always a chill.

He should be feeling happy, he told himself. The bulk of his work was done. He just had to write up all his notes. It was the tidying-up stage. He'd felt this way before when the 'Eureka' moment was over and the research that had been so hard-won was finished. Even if it was successful. Even if he knew he'd got it right (and he did know this), the challenge, the struggle, the excitement – everything that made it worthwhile – was over. Done with. Finished. Would there ever be another project just as exciting? Would this be his last? Would he have to spend the rest of his life twiddling his thumbs at home? The very idea made him fall into a dark hole of gloom. Usually Joe was around to cheer him up and suggest new projects which they could happily argue about over lots of cups of tea. But there was no Joe.

Pa did a few more stretches in the fresh summer air and went back inside the laboratory. For the moment he had a new and strange 'project' to explore. Himself.

'I think I might be rather lonely,' Amos Coggin said to the test tubes and the instruments that measured minute quantities of chemicals and the books that littered the table. 'In fact,' he continued, 'I think I'm homesick!'

This thought was quite a shock. Home, to Amos Coggin, was a place you returned to very happily and everyone was pleased to see you and you were pleased to see them, but then it was time to go. Time to get on. Time for work and solitude and Doing Something Useful.

'Sunday,' Amos said looking at the calendar hanging on the wall. And he thought of them all at *Dizzy Perch* – Ma snugged up reading a book,

Grandpa off in his workshop, maybe whittling a new animal, Lottie dressing up, Titch sorting through his beach glass, and Olly – dear Olly – probably cooking lunch. The sigh Amos Coggin gave seemed to come from the very bottom of his heart.

And so for fully ten seconds after Big Mac burst through the open door with Ma still roped to him, he thought that either he was seeing things or had developed some magical ability to produce holograms of people.

'Maisie!' he cried. 'Sweetheart! Best Love!'

'Dearest of Dear Hearts,' cried Ma, tears rolling down her cheeks as she reached out her arms towards him.

'Just you hold it there, Amos Coggin,' growled Big Mac, tightening his hold on Ma.

Pa reeled backwards. 'Big Mac Malone! My old school chum! What? Why? And just you let my wife go this minute.'

'Not so much your old school chum now, eh?' said Big Mac. 'All my life you've been ahead of me. Getting the prizes. Getting the jobs. Getting the girl. Now I've got a nice little exchange plan in mind. A deal.'

'A deal?' yelled Pa, raising his fists.

'Now you wouldn't want me to be hurting Maisie here, would you?' Big Mac lowered his voice to a whispered threat.

'Dear Heart!' pleaded Ma.

'What kind of a deal?' asked Pa, his face dark with anger. *Just how dangerous was this man?* he was wondering. *Did he have a knife? How had he got hold of Maisie in the first place?*

As if reading his thoughts, Ma said, 'Kidnapped. Got his sister to kidnap me. Cruel to horses. Kept me in a hayloft.' Fear, the journey to Auchterlaldy, the long haul up to the laboratory – all of it was making Ma hysterical.

Pa struggled to understand. It all sounded like one of the stories Ma loved to read. But clearly Big Mac – Maurice Mac Malone, as he'd been, and quite a pleasant boy once upon a long time ago – had become dangerous. Pa might be foolish in understanding his own feelings, or indeed anyone else's, but he recognised the fury of jealousy when he met it.

'The vaccine. Maisie for the vaccine.' Big Mac lolled against the wall, Ma held at his side. Pa winced to see that the rope was cutting into her wrist. He clenched his fists.

'The vaccine's gone!' shouted Pa. 'Gone. Gone to where you'll never get it!'

'But there's your results,' said Big Mac sweetly. 'In that book there, I expect.' He pointed to the large ledger on the table. 'All the results that will tell me how to make the vaccine. Forget the actual stuff, my old school chum, I'm more than happy to settle for "How To". How to make the vaccine! That'll do me very nicely.'

'Dear Heart – please!' begged Ma.

Grimly, Pa picked up the ledger.

He was holding it out towards Big Mac, and Big Mac was moving forward to take it, dragging Ma with him of course, when four figures – two boys, one wild, old woman and a young girl in leathers, all of them in such a hurry that they were almost tripping over each other – burst into the laboratory.

'Pa! Ma!' shouted Oliver.

And, 'Olly!' shouted his parents.

But Oliver wasn't looking at them. He'd spotted Big Mac.

'You!' Oliver shouted and, without a thought of danger, leapt at Big Mac and began pummelling him wherever he could reach, which somehow included Big Mac's rather large nose and a place in his tummy where it really hurt. Covering his head with his hands, Big Mac couldn't help but let go of Ma, who ran and flung herself in Pa's arms.

'It was you who wrote that ransom note,' yelled Oliver. 'I bet it was you who made Moll take Ma away. You! You! You!' shouted Oliver, accompanying each 'you' with a punch. For solidarity, Cezary thought he'd join in with a few kicks.

Then somehow it was A.C. Hennessy who took charge. Making herself very upright and fierce and using a voice that might make anyone jump to attention ('The Wrens,' Alicia whispered to Hattie, 'many moons ago') 'I take it,' she said, addressing Big Mac, who was now both pummelled and scared. 'I take it this is Anon,' the kidnapper of innocent women, of wives and mothers.'

'Only one wife and mother,' said Big Mac.

'And might I ask who you are?' Pa asked Alicia.

'She's A.C. Hennessy,' said Hattie. 'And I'm Hattie, in case anyone's interested.'

At which point Ma fainted, and had to be revived with a sniff of Pa's Tincture of Bygones.

'I suggest we tie him up with his own rope,' said Alicia. 'I've got rid of several villains like that.'

'She means in her stories,' Hattie explained.

'I'm very grateful for your help,' said Pa, 'though I really don't quite understand why you're here.'

So then Olly had to explain about Ma inviting A.C. Hennessy to come and stay, only it wasn't A.C. Hennessy who came but Moll with a horse called Amber. Oliver's story, interrupted over and over by Ma saying, 'Sorry, very very very sorry', got more and more garbled as he tried to explain how Titch and Lottie and Grandpa had become really fond of Moll, and how he and Cezary had gone to the library and . . .

'Enough!' said Pa. 'Enough that you've saved your mother and you've saved me and you've stopped this rogue getting his hands on my research. Oliver Coggin, you're a champion!'

Big Mac made a dash for the door.

'Oh no you don't,' said Alicia, sticking out a foot at just the right moment. 'If we're not going to tie him up, we could have him eaten by wolves,' she suggested. 'I did that in *Lucasta in the Wilderness*.'

'I don't think we're going to do either of those things,' said Pa.

'No wolves, I suppose,' said Hattie.

'We're going to let him go,' said Pa. 'I don't think my old school chum will ever trouble us again.'

'See!' Ma said to Big Mac. 'I told you, didn't I? Very, very bright and very, very foolish. Take your horrid old rope with you.'

Big Mac didn't need telling twice. He started down the track, battered and bruised in body and soul and with an ankle that was slowly swelling up.

Halfway down the track he could walk no more. He slid and rolled and bumped his way down to the bottom.

It was this big strange figure, grunting and groaning and waving his arms about that Stan, waiting by the bus, saw coming down the track.

It has to be him, Stan said to himself, *The kidnapper who snatched Oliver's Ma*. Stan smiled. What a very good job it was, he thought, that he'd taken the distributor cap out of that suspicious old jalopy, just in case it was the kidnapper's getaway car.

He sat quietly in the bus as Big Mac heaved himself into the car and tried to get it going. Stan munched another sandwich and waited. Waited until Big Mac abandoned the car and lurched over towards him.

'Want a lift,' Big Mac said.

Stan locked the driver's door, wound down

the window, said, 'Sorry pal, I'm full up,' and wound it back up.

For a moment Big Mac looked as if he was going to put a fist through the window. But somehow there was a look in Stan's eye that made him think better of it.

He began the long, slow walk along the empty road.

He might hitch a lift, Stan thought. *On the other hand, he might not.* And *not* was what he hoped.

Up in the laboratory, they all flopped at the table.

'Tea,' said Pa, 'and chocolate biscuits.'

'I suppose this is a sort of happy ending,' said Alicia a little doubtfully, 'only I'd really like a word with my imposter, and I did so want to visit *Dizzy Perch*.'

'So do I,' said Hattie.

'Well, I think we can arrange that,' said Pa. 'Let's all go home.'

'We can go on Stan's bus,' said Oliver.

So when Pa had doused the fire in the wood-burning stove with sand from a bucket, turned off the humming generator that gave the laboratory electricity, and, with the help of Oliver and Cezary, had packed up all his belongings – including his notebooks ('to work on when I'm home') – that's what they all did.

Alicia said she hoped Hattie wouldn't mind if she went on the bus with all the Coggins and Cezary. Hattie said she thought that would be a good idea and she would be much quicker if she didn't have to stop and look at beautiful views every five minutes. Perhaps if she got to Starwater, someone would show her the way to *Dizzy Perch*? And Oliver said he would. 'Because you brought the real A.C. Hennessy to us,' he said.

'It was a pleasure,' said Hattie.

Ma, one arm hooked in Pa's arm and the other arm hooked in Alicia's, looked radiant with happiness. 'Such Dear Hearts!' she said. Then they all trooped down the track, to where Stan was waiting.

'He's gone,' said Stan. 'Someone must have done something to that old jalopy of his. So he's walking!'

They all cheered.

'But I think I might have done something worse than harming an old jalopy,' said Stan.

'Good heavens, what?' asked Oliver.

Stan pointed to the furry animal on the ground. 'I think I killed it,' he said.

'Nonsense!' said Alicia, picking it up. 'That's my coat.'

Then Stan laughed and put his driver's cap on and they all got on the bus.

Hattie put on her helmet, mounted her bike, blew Alicia a kiss, and rode off.

'Starwater non-stop is it?' Stan asked

'Yes!' they all shouted.

P.S.

You'll be wondering about Moll and Amber.

Well, once Grandpa, Titch and Lottie had heard the full story from Ma and Oliver, and how Moll had never wanted to pretend to be A.C. Hennessy or kidnap anyone, and Pa (who you will remember was very bright and very foolish) said it was important to forgive people, that's what they did. And Titch said he forgave Amber too.

'She hasn't done anything wrong,' said Grandpa.

'She did,' said Titch. 'She carried Ma away. But I still love her.'

A.C. Hennessy got her wish and met her

imposter, Moll. They got on very well and when Alicia heard how Big Mac had threatened Amber, she said that she had a huge garden and several barns and sheds, any one of which could be a stable, so why didn't Moll come to live with her?

Moll said she'd be delighted because, actually, she'd begun writing some stories and maybe Alicia could help her. And Alicia said, 'Hurray, maybe I can stop and you can start.' Which was exactly what happened.

Pa stayed at home for at least three weeks before going back to his laboratory.

The biggest change was in Ma, who said it was time she took over the cooking from Oliver and maybe join that library in Brochmuir.

When Moll went to collect her things from the hayloft, the caravan had gone and so had Big Mac.

'Maybe he'll turn over a new leaf one day,' said Pa.

'Dear Heart,' said Ma.

'Very bright, very foolish,' she said to Oliver.

Oliver and Cezary had the rest of the summer to themselves. Mrs Tansley often saw the boys down at the harbour in Starwater. She told Mr Strut that Oliver looked very happy these days.

Hattie went back to Hubert & Busters and was made assistant editor after she introduced Mr Gadly to a new writer – Molly Malone.

Alicia did in fact write one more novel. It was called *The Imposter at High Craggs Hall.*

It was a flop.